CW01177266

While Hearts Count Our Forevers

While Hearts Count
Our Forevers

Hugh Major

DISJUNCT BOOKS

Published in 2025 by Disjunct Books
an imprint of Attar Books, New Zealand

Paperback ISBN 978-1-0670143-3-9
Hardcover ISBN 978-1-0670143-4-6

Copyright © Hugh Major 2025

Hugh Major's right to be identified as author of this work is asserted in accordance with Section 96 of the Copyright Act 1996.

All rights reserved. Except for fair dealing or brief passages quoted in a newspaper, magazine, radio, television or internet review, no part of this book may be reproduced in any form or by any means, or in any form of binding or cover other than that in which it is published, without permission in writing from the Publisher. This same condition is imposed on any subsequent purchaser.

Cover photo: Patrick Langwallner, Unsplash

Disjunct Books is published by Attar Books, a New Zealand publisher which focuses on work that explores today's spiritual experiences, culture, concepts and practices. For more information visit our website:

www.attarbooks.com

Hugh Major studied English and Philosophy at Auckland University and has taught these subjects at secondary schools, as well as English and Drama in both Scotland and Japan.

In his writing, Hugh explores new thinking in the fields of consciousness, science, spirituality and culture. Five times he has been a finalist in New Zealand's premiere Ashton Wylie Book Awards for writing in the mind, body, spirit genre. His published books include *Notes on the Mysterium Tremendum* (2010), *From Monkey to Moth* (2015), and *The Lantern in the Skull* (2019). All three were finalists in the Ashton Wylie Book Awards, with the third also a finalist in the 2020 International Independent Book Awards. This is his first published work of fiction.

Hugh lives in Matakana, New Zealand, with his partner Kirsty.

Contents

Dramatis Personae   9

Zeitgeist — Weltgeist   11

A Material Girl   61

Undoubtedly   117

Dramatis Personae

Zeitgeist — Weltgeist

Setting: 1798 to 1804, Jena University, Germany, where the Romantic philosophic movement had its beginnings.

Friedrich Schelling. Philosopher, advocate for Romanticism.

Caroline Schlegel. German intellectual.

August-Wilhelm Schlegel. Married to Caroline, professor of Sanskrit, co-founder of *Athenaeum*, a journal promoting Romantic thought.

Johann Fichte. Developed German idealism from Kant.

Novalis. Pen name of Georg von Hardenberg, writer, philosopher.

Johann Wolfgang von Goethe. Scientist and writer.

Friedrich (Fritz) Schlegel. August-Wilhelm's brother, co-founder of *Athenaeum*, married to Dorothea.

Georg Hegel. Idealist philosopher, author of *The Phenomenology of Spirit*.

A Material Girl

Setting: From 1644 in Paris during the English Civil War, to 1660 in England after the Restoration and crowning of Charles II, and later.

Margaret Cavendish (née Lucas). Philosopher, poet, scientist, fiction writer and playwright, the first woman to attend a meeting of the Royal Society of London.

William Cavendish, 1st Duke of Newcastle, later Marquess. Royalist commander, went into exile in France two years after the royalists lost the Civil War. Margaret's husband.

Queen Henrietta Maria. Married to Charles I, who was executed in 1649, then an exile in France until her son was crowned England's King Charles II in 1660.

Thomas Hobbes. Philosopher who wrote on history, theology, optics, ethics and political philosophy, tutored the Cavendish family.

René Descartes. The father of modern philosophy, a French mathematician and scientist.

Pierre Gassendi. French astronomer, philosopher, mathematician and Catholic priest.

Marin Mersenne. French scientist and mathematician, the father of modern acoustics, harmonics and music theory.

Royal Society of London. The world's oldest scientific academy, founded in 1660 when it was granted a royal charter by Charles II.

Undoubtedly

Setting: 1649 to 1650, Stockholm, Sweden.

René Descartes. Mathematician, scientist, philosopher.

Queen Christina. Twenty-three years old, sought to establish an intellectual academy in Stockholm, occasionally wore male clothing.

Francine Descartes. Descartes' daughter, died aged five.

Axel Oxenstierna. Queen Christina's Lord High Chancellor.

Pierre Chanut. French ambassador to Sweden, friend of Descartes.

Ebba Sparre. Queen Christina's lady-in-waiting and possibly lover.

Zeitgeist — Weltgeist

E VERY TIME FRIEDRICH looked across at Caroline, he felt himself in collusion with her discreet but powerful glances. With each he felt he was slipping into an abyss — of this woman, of Caroline. It wasn't just anyone's gaze; how rare to find this effortless interplay, of something deeply kindred, and somehow ordained. What else could it be but love? In this carriage, squeaking and rocking its way down the wintry forest track from Jena to Weimar, any disclosure of the wordless encounter had one unbending response: *verboten*.

He recalled the conversation just days before with Caroline's husband, August-Wilhelm Schlegel.

'What I value most highly about you,' Schlegel had said, 'are your ideas about art.'

'Thank you,' came Friedrich's polite response. The other remained unvoiced: What I value most highly about you is your wife.

He wondered how something so direct, light-hearted but cruel, could surface in his mind. Suppressed by his better nature, where did the thought come from? It lent weight to the idea the thinker is always somehow opaque to himself. These thoughts conveniently covered the most important idea — his frivolous comment was the truth.

Now, in the carriage, Friedrich Schelling felt both the joy of mutual attraction and the frustration that while the horses were taking them closer to Weimar, he wasn't getting any closer to Caroline Schlegel.

October, 1798. It was Germany's biggest cultural event of the year. Schiller's latest play, *Wallenstein*, was having its premiere in Weimar's freshly refurbished theatre. Friedrich, with the Schlegels and his colleague at Jena University, Johann Fichte, decided to forget the expense and hired a carriage for the sixteen-mile journey, lured by the promise of high drama in Goethe's magic citadel of the arts.

Goethe had been a prime mover in getting Friedrich to Jena. The young philosopher felt privileged at being mentored by him, Germany's high priest of literature. He also felt privileged to join Weimar's high society in a place of sumptuous interior design lit with hundreds of candles. Friedrich found the set and costumes of Schiller's play impressive, but the script *langweilig*, vapid and overworked.

Caroline was particularly bored, but had something else to watch during the performance: Friedrich Schelling. Twelve years younger than her, she was captivated by his penetrating gaze, strong frame, and the unruly but expressive waves in his hair. Did he know he had sensual lips? Was Caroline the first person to realise this on his behalf? As the actors declaimed and ranted she stole looks every so often, like taking sips of fine wine, the doses imparting their intoxicating effect. She was careful her glances wouldn't be seen by her husband, or the outspoken, obdurate Fichte. He might be part of their free-spirited group, but she sensed a moralistic streak in him.

During the intermission Schlegel went in search of Goethe. He returned with a plate of food.

'Impressed by the show?' he asked.

'Grand,' said Fichte.

'Bland,' said Caroline.

Schlegel was put out. 'You think so? Why?'

'A strange mix of exalted and puffed-up dialogue,' she replied.

'Anyway, I'll be staying here tonight,' said Schlegel.

'To work on the script?' Caroline countered with a brassy smirk, finishing her glass of champagne.

Schlegel ignored the remark. 'I'm meeting Goethe in the morning. Some publishing matters.'

'Good idea,' Fichte affirmed. 'I don't much fancy three hours in the carriage at this time of night. Besides, the champagne hasn't run out yet.'

Schlegel looked at Friedrich. 'If you'll be kind enough to accompany my wife back to Jena, Friedrich?'

'Certainly,' he said, imagining the horses with free rein, taking him and his beloved far to the south, to a new life in Ingolstadt or Regensburg.

Pitch darkness outside the theatre made it difficult to find their carriage. A cold wind was blowing in from the west, but their need for each other's company overrode any discomfort. Two weak lamps on the carriage gave the driver only a dim pool of light onto the road ahead, enough to reflect into the carriage, delineating Caroline's profile under her tumble of dark curls.

He took her hand, thinking of all the couples who had joined hands at the start of a coach trip, this reassuring contact remaining like a tactile pledge, while their minds, over the miles, took flight with memories or imaginings. For his own part, he felt this connection with Caroline as two vortices in a river coming together, blending.

As the carriage turned downhill into the forest, he imagined her husband being part of the same stream, an eddy at the other side of Caroline's powerful whirlpool. Perhaps their mutual attraction was working to diminish her involvement with Schlegel. Looked at this way, it was about physical forces, unrelated to ethics. Or was his metaphor just a clever way of absolving himself of betrayal?

The horses' hoofs kept up their easy rhythm. The carriage hadn't overturned, they weren't waylaid by robbers or an advance party of Napoleon's troops on the forest road, and Friedrich's hand was still holding Caroline's when the first lantern appeared at Johannistor in Jena.

Friedrich knew he belonged to the most sparkling intellectual scene in Germany. There was the vibrant Jena circle, and the university where the *weltanschauung* of the time — the idealist worldview, prioritising the human mind — was discussed and refined. Friedrich recognised Caroline as the most educated of the circle, able to converse in four languages, and proficient in mathematics, history, theology and English literature. He spent as much time as possible at August-Wilhelm and Caroline's house in Leutragasse.

One of these occasions sealed their union, without a word being spoken. He was caught in a thunderstorm, soaked through as rain rushed down inadequate gutters, pouring onto the cobbled pavement. Almost slipping, he ran to the Schlegel's door, hoping his knocking would be heard above the roar of the rain. Caroline opened the door, smiling at her drenched visitor. The look was freighted not just with mutual allurement, but inevitability. Her face with its knowing smile was surrounded by a cloudburst of curls the colour of raw sienna. So enchanting. So married. How long would he have to wait for her? Another year? Two years? He couldn't bear it.

Friedrich was negotiating a balance between this emotional bond and the controlled, predictable environment of Jena University. Teaching philosophy, writing up lectures and attending to his students was a means of keeping at bay the enticing image of Caroline and what he was to do about it. At the same time the ever affable and accommodating Schlegel personified Friedrich's own conscience — how could he ever make a cuckold of him?

Sitting in his office, Friedrich tried to shake himself out of the emotional impasse by going to the window where there was a view of the anatomy tower to the south. The day was clear but for two plumes of smoke from coal fires. They rose straight into the still air, twisting and dispersing. He must have absorbed traces of Fichte's ideas, still lingering in the air of his former office, which Friedrich now occupied. He remembered the recent conversation with his older colleague.

'How did you get here?' asked Friedrich.

'I could say on horseback,' Fichte replied. 'But there's a much grander answer: through Immanuel Kant.'

'No less.'

'I had been his student, and hoped he would assist me. So I brought him a manuscript. It was later published by him, in Königsberg. Of course people assumed he'd written it. It just took Kant to announce it was my work, and behold! — that's how I became a professor in Jena.'

'Well done,' said Friedrich.

There was a manic gleam in Fichte's eye.

'Yes, my conquest, and I am the conqueror!' he thundered, punching his palm with his fist.

It was bluster, but entirely in character. Fichte dressed like a soldier or renegade in rough, worn clothes, as though he had just engaged with a band of adversaries and put them to flight. With the overbearing manner came an intolerance of any ideological opponent.

Friedrich already knew he was to become that opponent. He had a different style at the lectern, more restrained, but no less cogent. Students queued to get in. They saw this young man of about their own age, attention directed towards them from between the twin candles lighting his notes, methodical, compelling.

Friedrich had heard the story: Fichte sweeping in like a squall, blowing away old ideas and replacing them with one central concept — the self. Opposed to the self, or the I, was the non-I, everything external and objective: beetles, birds, buildings and other people.

Friedrich saw it as a flawed system, but knew he had to be careful in attacking his colleague's theories, whether spoken or in print. He allowed himself to descend deep into Fichte's idea, then asked himself: Is my conclusion speculative drivel, or formulated by the stable marriage of intuition and reason? To Fichte he wanted to say: 'You suggest a unified reality, but isn't nature an integral participant in experience? Isn't human experience an indivisible whole? It is not only the intellect that reveals the world but the whole person, intuitive, sensory, emotional, imaginative.'

He pictured Fichte's expostulation in response as taking a long draw on his meerschaum pipe, then filling the room with an acrid cloud of counter-argument.

In a love relationship — his own with Caroline — he felt two souls merge into one. Wasn't this the perfect rebuttal to Fichte? It was part of the Jena circle's belief system, best expressed by the poet Novalis, who saw subject and object as collaborators in a reciprocal relationship. Friedrich was in full agreement with Fichte's philosophy of *freiheit*, freedom, but could not abide a world divided into I and Not-I. With Caroline, Friedrich felt a coalescing, one with the other. There was a divinity in unified reality. A culture informed this way will be balanced, energised, and able to combine both scientific and artistic thought.

~

> *Come, gentle night, come, loving, black-browed night,*
> *Give me my Romeo; and when he shall die,*
> *Take him and cut him out in little stars,*
> *And he will make the face of heaven so fine*
> *That all the world will be in love with night*
> *And pay no worship to the garish sun.*
> *O, I have bought the mansion of a love,*
> *But not possessed it, and, though I am sold,*
> *Not yet enjoyed; so tedious is this day*
> *As in the night before some festival*
> *To an impatient child that has new robes*
> *And may not wear them.*

'Well-spoken, Caroline,' said Novalis, opening his eyes after the recital, the curls in his long hair burnished gold by an oil lamp on the table.

The young Auguste, sitting cross-legged on the worn percale of her favourite chair, asked:

'Who is waiting for nightfall?'

'Shakespeare's Juliet,' said Caroline. 'I'm translating the play.'

'Those lines,' said Novalis, '*I have bought the mansion of a love, But not possessed it* —'

'She's waiting for consummation.'

Friedrich didn't miss Caroline's glance.

'The metaphor of night,' said Novalis, 'it suits perfectly. I'm using it in my work.'

'I noticed the other image,' said Friedrich, 'of the child with party robes she's yet to wear.'

'It describes my daughter,' said Caroline, who was the only one standing: hostess, overseer and performer. She strolled around the table to Auguste, kissing her on the forehead.

'Unlikely,' said Schlegel. 'At fourteen your daughter's not going to entertain any wooers.'

'Juliet was fourteen,' observed Caroline.

'Even so, it's more like her mother's game.'

'I'm sure you're right,' said Caroline, continuing around the table to where Friedrich was sitting, balancing a piece of herring on his fork. Her hand touched his neck, tenderly, not an unusual gesture for Caroline, who was demonstrative in her affections. Friedrich couldn't enter easily into Caroline's games of repartee, but loved her spontaneous advances, even in full view of her husband.

That was her style: malapert, always ready to vanquish a smart remark with a smarter one of her own. And why should she hide her feelings for Friedrich? Didn't everyone here at Leutragasse know how close they were?

Friedrich had a suggestion. 'We've listened to Shakespeare. Now I want to hear poetry written closer to home.'

'You can only mean Novalis,' replied Caroline.

'Alright then,' said the poet, brushing his curled curtain of hair away with lissom fingers, then picking up a leather-bound, handwritten book. A hush fell across the table.

At no grave can weep
Any who love and pray.
The gift of love they keep,
From none can it be taken away.
To soothe and quiet his longing,
Night comes and inspires —
Heaven's name round them thronging
Watch and guard his heart.

Have courage, for life is striding
To endless life along;
Stretched by inner fire,
Our sense becomes transfigured.
One day the stars above
Shall flow in golden wine,
We will enjoy it all
And as stars we will shine.

For Friedrich there was no one like the messianic Novalis, no one at Jena who could be called a poet, philosopher and mystic. He was lanky, with limpid skin and an otherworldly look. Schooled in medicine, mathematics, chemistry, electricity and mineralogy, he was nothing like these elements and systems, defined instead by his poetry, his celebrated *Hymns of the Night*.

Friedrich knew the hymns must have been driven by the tragic attachment Novalis had formed some three years before. Novalis had fallen for the waif-like Sophie von Kühn, and they became secretly engaged. She was only thirteen, sickly and feverish, but he loved her with a passion. He might have sensed their destiny, but embraced it anyway, Sophie's unspoken message being: 'With me you're doomed.' Was it necessary for this misfortune to stalk the romantic poet, waiting to fathom the writer's deep desires? Perhaps, because it was only a year before Sophie fell ill, dying in Jena.

Friedrich saw not only the lost love for Sophie inspiring Novalis's poetry, but the sense of a kindred soul separated by death and thus able to be reached through his own departure from this world. Mercifully, the death-wish lasted only a few years before the tide turned and he regained his love of life, his poetic gift tested through adversity.

∼

At ten on a Sunday night Leutragasse was quiet except for the bakery getting started two doors down. Novalis and Fichte had left, Schlegel had gone up to his study, and his stepdaughter, Auguste, was in bed. Back in the parlour, Friedrich was with Caroline at the table. She was wearing a dress dyed dark blue from powdered indigo, a blue as deep as the ocean. They sat in the warm pool of a single candle flame, just bright enough to see them both reflected in the convex of a copper ladle at rest on the damask of the table cover — their own world, right to the round horizon.

'You were going to tell me about Königstein,' he said.

'You're sure you want to know? It was six years ago.'

'I want to know everything about you.'

The candle-glow flickered for a moment across her cheek.

'Just out of Mainz, Auguste and I were stopped on the road. I was identified as a sympathiser of the French Revolution, and arrested. They were right, of course. But punishment for supporting the cause of freedom? We felt the animosity, both of us, when we were taken away in a carriage. It was pelted with stones. And how fitting: at Königstein we were going to be surrounded by stone, oppressed by it. We arrived at the fortress and were put in a dark room with a few other women. *Schmuddelig*, said Auguste — yes, filthy, smelly. Who has the right to lock up a blameless seven-year-old in a place like that? I felt for her, my daughter, before anything else. I felt as though the stones of the fortress were in my stomach, constantly weighing on me, a granitic meal. I imagined Auguste threatened by this hard, immovable material, because she was so young, soft and delicate, cast into the wrong realm. She was so full of life and thirsting for new experience in the outer world. It was criminal to imprison her. Confinement for an adult is another thing. I hoped I had built enough resilience to endure the immobility, the blank and unyielding walls, the meagre portions of food pushed under the door. They kept us alive on tasteless potatoes, if we were lucky. And water was a treat, because there had always been problems getting water that high into the fortress from such a deep well below. The prisoners were their last consideration. Königstein's custodians were known more for cruelty than compassion.'

For a moment Caroline just sat, staring into the shadows.

'Only once did I see the real world outside. I saw the Elbe gliding quietly below through fields and forest. I cried for the beauty of it.'

Friedrich looked away, shaking his head. His comment sounded trite: 'To be deprived of light, fresh air and nature . . .'

'Then it started getting cold. I've never hugged Auguste so long and so hard.'

'How did you occupy your mind?'

'I recited poems I had learnt, lines from plays, parts of Shakespeare, all to myself, feeling the passion in them like a kind of antidote against the heartless oppressors who had put us there. But then — I'm sorry Friedrich, but you have to know — I was pregnant. He was a French soldier... Well, does it matter who? It helped the stone-walled room was so gloomy it hid my condition. But I was starting to panic. I tried with letters, tried reaching anyone with authority, to get us out of that place. I started to fall ill. Would both of us die in there? Auguste was so sweet. She was my constant helper, even cheerful, if you can believe it. They started bringing in more prisoners — less potato, less water to go round. I remember thinking, I can't last another week. Then someone heard my voice. After four months we were released. My soon-to-be husband helped. And my brother.'

'Did anyone discover the pregnancy?'

'Auguste and I had to keep moving. I had the baby. It was a son. He was fostered out. Few knew about this. They couldn't know I was an erring sister — is that the term? Now you know me, Friedrich. A whore to the French invaders, begetter of a bastard child.'

It sounded like a line she had used before, taken from the mouths of moralistic slanderers. He saw in her eyes the mix of defiance and self-reproach.

'It makes me love you more,' he said.

'Much more?'

'From the scalp to the soles.'

Novalis prepared to read while his friends sat around the fire in Caroline's parlour at Leutragasse. Caroline was rearranging a vase of elder flowers on the table. Friedrich sensed such moments with the poet might be fleeting, so gave him his full attention.

Infinite and mysterious
Thrills through me a sweet trembling,
As if from far there echoed thus
A sigh, our grief resembling:
The dear ones long as well as I,
And sent to me their waiting sigh.

'Dreamy,' said Schlegel, as he gazed at flames licking around the grate.

'Amorous,' said Caroline, doling out what she liked to call a kelch, or chalice, of vegetable broth.

'It's just as well Fichte isn't here tonight,' said Friedrich. 'Novalis, I'm interested in your view of his I and Not-I. Fichte starts from logic, but you start from lyricism.'

'Just a warning, you two,' said Caroline, taking a sip of her steaming soup. 'If this gets too convoluted, I'm going to be silly.'

'My position is straightforward, Caroline,' said Novalis. 'Perhaps language is the I and imagination is the Not-I, because it reaches outwards. I engage with philosophy not to chop logic, but to know myself better.'

'Commendable,' said Schlegel, raising his cup.

Novalis looked at Friedrich.

'To take a leaf from your book, Friedrich, our quest is for oneness, and science has to be married to art, poetry and philosophy.'

'Magical realism,' observed Schlegel. 'Isn't that it? Where feeling comes first?"

'Our cause is Romanticism,' said Novalis. 'We place emotion over rationality, as you know, and —'

' — affirm individual freedom?' completed Friedrich.

They were standing next to the Saale's swirling currents, the Jägersburg ridge catching the first dawn light. Jena was quiet, before the tradespeople got to work, before the wagons were hitched to horses and street-life commenced for the day. Friedrich knew the exact direction of Leutragasse where his loved one was probably still sleeping — warm, undisturbed, oblivious of him out on the border of the town.

Huddled in their overcoats both felt the biting cold, but it was worth it for the solitude. Their clouding breaths were sentences, briefly visible before dissolving.

'It was not in stolen looks that I knew, but in the way you've been lifted from heaviness to weightlessness. It's in your body, in your eyes,' said Novalis, clearly no fool when it came to divining the attraction between Friedrich and Caroline.

'And how could you be sure it was Caroline?'

'She's the same when in your presence.'

An image of her face, the familiar one from an amalgam of memories, jumped into his mind, then deliquesced.

'With her I'm drawn beyond myself.'

'Isn't that the mission of being human?' said Novalis. 'I should say you'll have the gift of each other and to seize it while you can, but . . .'

'But?'

'The Schlegel's have pledged themselves to each other.'

'I think — that's only a formality.'

'But you threaten the sanctity of marriage.'

'Do I threaten it when Caroline is in love with me? You said she was the same when in my presence.'

'Have you thought of using this tension to write?'

'I want to use it to act, but . . .' Friedrich sensed the offer to swerve away from the moral issue. 'I'm interested in your poetry. Not just aesthetically, but the idea that art shows what cannot be said.'

Friedrich was taken back to a set of portraits he had seen at the City Hall in Leipzig, and the artists' ability to record what was beyond language. Only those paintings capturing the essence and presence of the subject would qualify, transcending mere paint and finding something deeply human.

He looked at Novalis, now in profile. Just as the inexpressible gleamed between his lines of verse, so did facets of an elusive self appear in his face, then melt into each other.

Friedrich knew this was the direction his work was going: *The Philosophy of Art*.

Schlegel had taken his step-daughter Auguste with him to supervise the printing of his literary magazine, *Athenaeum*. Caroline had decided she and Friedrich would meet at Paradise Park south of Jena, on the banks of the Saale. They'd make their way there separately, so there would be no tittle-tattle about Mrs Schlegel consorting with an unmarried man.

Friedrich took the long way through Saalter towards the river east of the town, following, for a time, the departing mail coach. He passed a gateway with rosettes chiselled into the stone at either side. A nice symbolism — the rose as love and purity binding two souls, himself and Caroline. Then the gateway... to what?

They found a spot under the trees where Caroline unwrapped a picnic lunch of silverside with gherkins and wine. It was quiet. No-one else could be seen on the curving pathway.

'It's your turn,' said Caroline.

'To fill your glass?'

'To tell me of your life.'

'Once upon a time I ventured into Thuringia, where I met a passionate, dark-haired beauty named Caroline.'

'I knew the wine would make you talk. Now, tell me the story.'

'But that's the best part of it.'

'Friedrich!'

'My story isn't as dramatic or hazardous as your own. My father was a theologian. He studied in Göttingen.'

'Do you know who he studied under?'

'Yes, it was Professor Michaelis.'

'My father.'

'What?'

'You heard. My father taught theology at Göttingen.'

'That's astonishing.'

'No, appropriate,' she said. 'I too can teach a Schelling all there is to know,' her hand reaching for his chest, feeling the warmth, then gracefully withdrawing.

He could see a small scattering of freckles disappearing into the sleeve of her light muslin dress. She continued:

'Now, come on, next please. Languages?'

'Latin and Greek. My father had his sights set on my joining the church, but Tübinger Stift, the seminary where I was educated, was a grim, regimented place. It would never make a clergyman of me. Anyway, I wasn't challenged at all. I wanted to be at home among my father's books, teaching myself.'

'That makes you sound bookish, studious, inward.'

'I suppose that's right. Perhaps it makes me a bit tedious.'

'No, Friedrich, your eyes have a blue fire of intelligence. You're my liebling. I love you.'

'The feeling is,' his lips only inches from Caroline's, 'most definitely, mutual.'

'So now,' she said, checking the path from left to right, 'you should kiss me.'

They kissed to the subdued sound of the Saale's currents, then a soughing of leaves overhead. Even Caroline, with her propensity to blatantly flirt with him, felt they shouldn't push their luck.

'I think it's time I retraced my steps from our bower of bliss.'

'You sound like a Romantic poet. Since we're purists for propriety, I'll wait here, as arranged.' Quieter, and closer to her, he said: 'I need time to savour our kiss.'

'A very good afternoon, Professor Schelling,' she said with exaggerated effusiveness.

'Goodbye, Mrs Schlegel,' he replied.

Caroline took her basket, tossed her curls with a flick of the head, and descended to the pathway.

After she had gone Friedrich was left watching the eddies in the river, how they poured, swirled, rippled and drew apart.

～

Friedrich didn't need to read more than a paragraph of the memorandum to realise the state of affairs at both the university and among the Jena circle had completely altered. This was a blow against freedom of expression, but also a victory for unquestioning orthodox belief.

Sitting in his office, there was little light to read by. He squinted at the paper, needing to revisit the condescending part where the much-esteemed 'Elector of Saxony' — of such lofty heights he could take part in choosing the Holy Roman Emperor — 'has decreed that Johann Fichte is hereby accused of atheism.'

Friedrich thumped his fist on the desk, sending a cloud of dust into the air. 'All Fichte has said is there is an ethical basis to the concept of God and that we require no other,' he said in full lecture theatre volume, to the empty room.

Once he had calmed down, Friedrich considered the repercussions for Jena's professors. They were out on a limb. No-one would want to side with those who openly challenged authority.

His friends were in agreement.

'Anti-intellectual,' said Novalis. 'It's straight censorship.'

'They're policing our thoughts,' declared Schlegel. 'We have to counter-attack.'

'Now he's launched that into the mainstream,' observed Caroline, 'he can't get out of the current.'

Seeing Fichte near the lecture hall, his face red as beetroot and about to explode, Friedrich felt it best to keep the man at a distance.

The following day Schlegel presented the news update.

'Johann's reaction to the charge has been forceful and immediate,' he said. 'He's incapable of grovelling, so he's attacked his accusers instead.'

'Well done,' said Caroline.

'He's saying they're guilty of *schikanierung*.'

'Harassment,' said Novalis. 'That's exactly what it is.'

Schlegel smiled, enjoying his role as town cryer.

'He's even said they are themselves atheists for — what were his words? — "Following a set of rigid dogma while being oblivious to the inner flame of the divine."'

Friedrich could picture the defiant light in Fichte's eye.

Just a fortnight later Fichte took action. Aware of his own popularity and value to Jena University, he played his trump card, warning his adversaries he would resign.

The resignation was accepted.

When there was time to think clearly about the scandal, Friedrich could see the hazardous game his colleague had been playing. Life was a balancing act. Events would conspire against you, or so it seemed, demanding some kind of response or choice. The ousted Fichte was in trouble. He had no job, no income, and no-one was going to risk hiring him.

'I want to tell you something momentous,' said Goethe.

'That you're moving from Weimar to Jena?'

'I hardly need to. Jena is a refuge from my home and responsibilities in Weimar.'

Friedrich felt important, strolling the botanical gardens whose development Goethe had supervised, the poet now pointing out a row of silk-vine displaying crimson flowers.

'I'm sorry. We diverted from the momentous —'

'Ah, yes. The fact is, I'm turning fifty next week.'

'Then I should congratulate you.'

'Well, I've evaded arrows and gunfire, penury and plague so far,' he announced to some exotic red trumpets of amaryllis. 'And something else: you bright young things are good for maintaining my vitality.'

'The feeling's reciprocated.'

'Anyway, I'm heading into the latter phase, Friedrich. At least death will rid me of my ever-fattening hulk.'

'I imagine death to be a different reality, radically reorganised.'

'It will have to be more than pleasant to emulate this thuja, my botanical emerald,' he said, letting it brush across his palm. 'Perhaps you can see why I've worked to establish this place. The plants are of scientific interest, and beneficial to the senses. I'd always thought it was this act of observation that was the source of knowledge about the world.'

'It is,' said Friedrich. 'But Fichte would hold that everything about your thuja — its size and spread, its colour and smell, its seeds and whole genus — starts in the mind. I believe it's a synthesis of the two: the mind, but also observation. In other words, it comes from experience, which covers both.'

They had arrived at a row of red roses.

'I write poetry among these trees, plants and roses,' Goethe observed. 'If poetry was only about observation, then I couldn't write anything. I have to wait for something unobserved that only poetry can put into words.'

'There's something vital and mysterious in the rose that can't be explained by facts and figures,' Friedrich added. 'It's an active process.'

'Nature in motion is what you're saying?'

'Yes. A living, interconnected unity.'

~

Schlegel's brother, Fritz, returned to Jena from Berlin, arriving on a fresh wave of scandal.

Friedrich could tell from the outset they wouldn't get on. Fritz (the nickname sounding like an Alsatian dog) still carried a torch for Caroline. He would stare at her, tenderly, oblivious of his own lover, Dorothea, by his side. Friedrich had learned of aspersions cast about *Lucinde*, Fritz's titillating tale that bore a remarkable resemblance to the love affair between himself and Dorothea.

'The only thing more upsetting than being the subject of rumour,' Fritz had said, 'is failing to be the subject of rumour.'

To those who cautiously suggested *Lucinde* was excessive, Fritz claimed kinship with the Jena circle: 'We're all splendid outlaws.'

The couple were assigned to a garret room in the Leutragasse house.

From the outset Friedrich could see Dorothea was crushed by Caroline, who had everything she lacked: an advanced education, confidence, articulacy, aplomb, attractiveness and sartorial flair. Friedrich felt hard-hearted to even think it, but there was something plain, dumpy and graceless about Dorothea — or was it just by comparison with the radiant Caroline? Her eyes had a squinty look, her lips pursed as if in constant distaste, and her heavy brows maintained a sternness no matter what emotion issued from within.

He wondered if her soul had wrought these features into her face over the years, perhaps from her loveless life with the banker she had been forced to marry aged fourteen, as Caroline had told him, quietly, before their arrival. But he found it instinctive to judge Dorothea on appearances, just as he would anyone else. The offence was to express such judgements. With the closeness and volatility of the circle at their Leutragasse headquarters, any such opinions should be kept well-hidden.

More than once he had seen Fritz's attention on Caroline turn into a leer. Friedrich could have stepped away, freeing himself from the jealousy and status games. But he couldn't live without Caroline. Also, this was Schlegel's house, and his wife had hegemony over her own parlour.

Fritz and Dorothea brought worrying news. Novalis was ill with stomach pains and coughing up blood. 'I'm firing a red constellation into my handkerchief,' were the poet's words. His doctor recommended fresh air, and even a trip south to warmer weather in Italy, but winter was crawling down from the north.

Friedrich valued his ideas and enjoyed his readings, but still couldn't square the poet's moral stand against his love for Caroline with the Romantics' creed that love rules the world. It certainly ruled the life of Novalis. Friedrich put the thought aside. He was enjoying the aroma of Caroline's spaetzle dumplings.

When they were brought to the table Auguste, in a cool grey linen dress modified by her mother from one of her own, was the first to descend, grabbing the largest. Schlegel was ruffled.

'Save some for the rest.'

'I have.'

'He's right,' said Caroline, with a cough, 'it's rude to snatch.'

'I know you'd rather I starved.'

'Don't exaggerate.'

'Can you make spaetzle, Dorothea?' asked Schlegel.

'Well —'

'No, she can't,' said Fritz.

'Hers taste like regurgitated dough,' whispered Auguste as she passed Caroline.

'What was that?' asked Fritz.

'Nothing.'

Friedrich laughed.

'What's so funny?' asked Fritz.

'Nothing.'

'Anyway, they're so tasty,' Fritz affirmed, selecting his own. 'Caroline's always had a way with baking.'

'Yes, Caroline,' added Dorothea, 'you're such a competent provider.'

'I do my best.' Caroline aimed a forced smile in her direction.

'Mother is a competent provider,' repeated Auguste, not having seen Caroline's friendly grimace. Then, assuming a clipped, haughty air for theatrical effect: 'A proficient preparer. A qualified equipper.' She took another bite.

Dorothea wanted to say 'Cheeky little madam,' but turned and glared at the wall instead.

Friedrich waited till last before taking a spaetzle. Now that Fritz and Dorothea were added to the family at Leutragasse he felt lowest-ranked, a mere spectator on the verbal action. The only talk he wanted was with Caroline — quiet, one-to-one, intimate. Why should he feel reprehensible for having followed his heart? It seemed ironic that the only one who engaged with him as an equal, aside from Caroline, was Schlegel. So it wasn't at all contrary when Schlegel called him aside later and took him upstairs to his study.

Friedrich had never seen a study so ordered: shelves with books perfectly placed as to matching heights and binding, journals all named and numbered on their spines, freshly-dusted inkwells, letters in boxes catalogued alphabetically, a desk clear of clutter but for a notebook, tray of pens and sheets of guillotined paper. He could see it as an ordered haven, away from the disordered parlour of endless visitors. And from Caroline.

There was always a touch of formality in Schlegel's dress and speech, a finicky attitude in his editing of work for publication, but also a strong sense of fairness in his dealings with others. Was it this conviction, Friedrich wondered, that tipped the balance to free Caroline from the Königstein fortress? And now, was Schlegel going to use the same certitude and ethical stand to warn him off Caroline?

'You've probably noticed that Caroline is unwell. It's not just her cough. She's also prone to fevers and headaches.'

'I've noticed,' said Friedrich. 'I was hoping it was only this run of cold weather.'

'The stress of feeding and entertaining an increasing number of guests can't be helping. It can get quite tense downstairs. But she's not one to complain.'

'I could reduce my visits.'

'No, not at all,' said Schlegel. 'You're the least negative influence. What I'm proposing is a trip away from all her commitments here. I've just received a reply from a doctor in Bamberg. He's happy to have Caroline in his care for a few weeks.'

This seemed to Friedrich like a fait accompli. He was concerned for Caroline's health, but to be absent from her for so long? His mind was already forming plans for getting to her in Bamberg incognito. Perhaps as a priest. Or a mortician, the coffin full of flowers for —

'Auguste should accompany her,' said Schlegel, interrupting his thoughts. 'And you, of course. The only part of this plan I can't resolve is how to coordinate your arrival in Bamberg by different routes, or times, given the sensitivity of . . .'

'I understand. Leave that to me. You've been very considerate. And thank you.'

Schelling stifled the cry of triumph after closing the office door.

⁓

It was raining on his next visit to Leutragasse. Alerted by low voices as he entered from the courtyard, he decided it was best to exercise caution and stealth. After hanging his coat at the back door he waited, not wanting to break in on a private discussion or disturb any intimacy. Then he saw Fritz and Caroline near the fire, in close conversation.

Friedrich wouldn't forget their combined posture. They were sitting side by side on a narrow upholstered settle, Caroline with Fritz's hand in hers, both looking intently at each other, speaking softly because of their close proximity. So engaged were they in this cosy heart-to-heart that neither sensed his presence just outside the door, his beam of attention on them, his possessiveness over Caroline so amplified he had to turn and just as discreetly exit.

Fears bounded up behind him — that they were lovers, that they had rediscovered each other after Fritz's time in Berlin, that Dorothea was really just a second string and could be relinquished at a moment's notice.

Then the philosopher in him presented the counter-argument, that Caroline was naturally demonstrative and affectionate, so with Fritz this quality (or was it attribute?) should be no different. Also, he couldn't be more certain of Caroline's love for him. It wasn't just coquetry on her part, it was real. Finally, did he trust her? He rejected the resolution of 'I have to trust her', and settled instead on 'I trust her'.

Their trip away couldn't come soon enough.

Friedrich left Jena on his own, waiting for them in the small town of Saaffeld, at the crossroads of their coordinated, clandestine journey. Schlegel accompanied Caroline and Auguste to Saalfeld, then continued alone to Leipzig. Still cautious, the lovers remained divided for the second half of the journey, through the Thüringer

Wald to Bamberg. Yet despite their best efforts to be discreet, tongues were wagging back in Jena. Friedrich knew the rumours and could imagine it all:

'You know the real reason they've gone to Bamberg, don't you?' says Dorothea.

'I've a few ideas. Why?'

'It gives Caroline time to organise Auguste's marriage to Friedrich Schelling.'

'Why would she do that?'

'Think about it. It's a formality that gives Caroline better access to him.'

'I'm dubious,' says Fritz. 'But time will tell.'

'Dubious about that conniving bitch? The sad thing is, Auguste is being groomed by her mother for the same role. The temptress. Notice how Auguste is getting interested in stylish dresses? It's all her mother's fault.'

If Dorothea had shadowed them to Bamberg, she'd have learnt that Friedrich had booked a suite of rooms overlooking the river Regnitz, each with its own high dormer window opening to the town. The suites enabled them to be close, but, to a casual observer, independent of each other.

Auguste knew exactly what was going on, teasing her mother and Friedrich at any opportunity. Now they were like a married couple, Auguste softened her once antagonistic attitude to Friedrich, but was always ready for a verbal joust.

'That skimming of cream from the jug has given you a white moustache,' observed Friedrich.

'You're only jealous because you can't grow one.'

'No, I'd prefer not to have a wire-brush on my top lip.'

Leaving the room, Auguste said, 'I'll leave you two lovebirds alone. Then, softly, and striking her mother's posture: 'My door will be ajar after ten.'

'That's quite enough, Auguste.'

'You'll want him in with you though, won't you Mother?'

'Auguste!'

'I heard you last night,' she said. 'Your laughter was in French.'

Friedrich laughed, then they all did.

Away from Leutragasse they could relax and enjoy somewhere new. The only person who would have stood in their way, Schlegel, had granted them this opportunity to be together.

When on his own, Friedrich went for walks around the town. He was out on the perimeter. Suddenly, sweeping into his vision, was a flock of lapwings, turning, billowing, then pouring as if through a gap. So arresting was the display that it could have been a flown announcement, an avian revelation, had he the ability to read it.

Where did the feeling come from that these appearances might portend something? Did it come down to the size of the flock, how and where they swooped, then concentrated, turned and dispersed? Or was it all just superstition? Shouldn't he just enjoy the spectacle? But he couldn't shake the feeling that these blacksmith lapwings were trying to tell him something.

In his walks he always tried to include the Alt Rathaus, sitting mid-stream, at right angles to the Obere Brucke bridge. Such bold but playful architecture was designed for its constant and intimate proximity to the river. This human artefact had a reassuring solidity and presence, unchanged from day to day, year to year, while the river of time rushed incessantly beneath.

Always drawn to the river, his eye was caught once more by the eddies, just like those of the Saale he'd watched after the picnic with Caroline. Little maelstroms hustled around each other in the moving skein of current. They were all in there somewhere — Caroline, Auguste and himself, launched into the overall flow, together but self-directed and compelled by the same surrounds.

Change and flow. What could be waiting for them further downstream?

Friedrich imagined becoming Auguste's stepfather. It had been difficult at first, but now they were *kumpels* — pals. Forthright and intellectually supple, like her mother, he wondered if poetry would be Auguste's future path.

'As for you, Mister Friedrich Professor.'

'What about me?'

' Without a hairdresser.'

'Do you think I'm slovenly?'

'Nonsense, my mother needs to run her fingers through your locks, sit by the fire, darn your socks . . .'

~

With Caroline's health much improved, all three moved on to the spa town of Bocklet. It was a small place, feeling like a distant outpost. As the carriage wound its way through a grove of trees towards an imposing stone building, the sunlight slanting across its roof, Friedrich noticed a vital spark had returned to Caroline's eyes — the promise of their life to come, and their love for each other, all inherent in that look.

He couldn't pinpoint what part of the journey was responsible for the change in her, or why she had been singled out. He knew from his own experience these things just take hold from somewhere so deep and unexpected there can be no way to reverse the tide.

As they unloaded their luggage Auguste felt the first cramps in her stomach. Caroline said it must have been the bumping and swaying of their carriage on the rough road, and suggested she lie down to settle herself.

It wasn't that easy. Auguste's abdominal pains continued through the night. Friedrich was woken by Caroline, distraught.

'She's had to keep . . . relieving herself . . . and there's blood.'

By the time they summoned a doctor Auguste had turned feverish. The doctor tried to impose a confident and businesslike manner over his vexation at the girl's condition. First he administered laudanum with acacia gum, then a vegetable compound he explained would help void the bowels.

Friedrich was sceptical. But not being a physician he could hardly object. Or suggest an alternative. They were caught in a *zugzwang* of crucial but ill-informed choices.

'It seems wrong to use drugs that purge the system when the body is already doing so,' he said to Caroline when they were alone.

'I'm sure you're right. But what can we do?'

'My instincts tell me to trust the body's ability to heal itself.'

'But she's been given a purgative.'

'I think it was a mistake.'

Friedrich could see tears welling in his lover's eyes. He said:

'She's taken it and it's too late. But opium will help. She'll be able to sleep.'

'. . . fresh food, and water . . .' added Caroline, mechanically.

Auguste's condition worsened.

'Am I dying?'

'My sweet girl.'

'I don't want to lose you,' she said, weakly, eyeing both of them, shivering under the blankets.

Friedrich remembered what Caroline had said about her daughter — 'cast into the wrong realm.' She was like a seraph mislaid by angelic beings, but with bonds of love fastening her to this place. He could see an improving picture for Auguste just before the illness caught her. Caroline was a happier mother after her time away from Jena, and Friedrich was a new father figure she had not only accepted, but had grown to love. Why was this time of contentment and promise so short? What had conspired to end it?

While Caroline mopped the sweat from her daughter's brow and encouraged her to drink, it was decided to summon the physician from Bamberg who had brought Caroline back to health. But both were alarmed at the rate of Auguste's decline, and the doctor at least forty-eight hours away. Friedrich would never forget the look on Auguste's face — though she was in an opiate lethargy he could see the frightened girl underneath.

Through daylight and candlelight Caroline never left her daughter's side, beseeching in whispers her Bamberg doctor to arrive and perform a life-saving miracle.

It was too late. After just over a week fighting dysentery, Auguste succumbed.

They both felt the moment, the pulse of it. To Friedrich, it was as if the young girl, projected so uniquely, so benevolently into the objective world, had grown wings and flown deep inside herself.

Caroline felt expunged from reality. Though her heart was still beating, her whole being was following Auguste's spirit into the dark, desperate to find her. But mother and daughter were lost to each other, permanently. She couldn't stop crying.

Friedrich was in shock:

'If only I'd summoned the doctor from Bamberg sooner.'

When August-Wilhelm heard the news he travelled straight to Bamberg, where Caroline and Friedrich were waiting. Friedrich remained there with Schlegel and Caroline for three months. Nothing could console Caroline after her loss, while Friedrich couldn't exonerate himself from the culpability of delay. Always the question: 'If only …'

Friedrich fell prey to *schwermut*, a heaviness of heart that persisted for weeks, deepened by Schlegel's and Caroline's grief, not helped by a series of storms that descended from the Thuringia Wald. With each successive day his spirits dropped further. He couldn't find his former self. Since suicide provided the option of a way out, it assumed a profound significance. Given this momentous downturn, was his life now worth living? What kept alive the desire to go on?

Novalis had already been there. His *Hymns to the Night* supplied Friedrich with a context to loss, to the dark hollow he was living in, where the vital source of life seemed out of reach. Applying the hymns to Auguste, she had crossed the threshold into night, as Sophie had done for Novalis. Paeans to the night, to death, were part of the spirit of Romanticism. Both Auguste and Sophie had become, through love and their crossing over, a conduit to the divine. The spur was there in Novalis's *Longing for Death*:

> *Into the bosom of the Earth!*
> *Out of the light's dominions!*
> *Death's pains are but the bursting forth*
> *Of Glad departure's pinions!*
> *Swift in the narrow boat,*
> *Swift to the heavenly shore we float!*

Caroline was to spend another four months away with Schlegel. For Friedrich, the part of him that wrote and delivered lectures knew he would be able to tolerate the time away. However, saying goodbye to Caroline was another matter entirely.

The formal leave-taking in Schlegel's presence was starchy and mechanical. But after he had gone the lovers retreated further, to the dim corner of a hallway, where Friedrich saw Caroline's eyes, for so long watery with grief, now ignited with the fervour he remembered. Weren't their bodies separable but their hearts forever joined? Of course they were!

Caroline's hand was behind his neck, holding his cheek against her own.

'Only now,' he whispered, 'with this parting, do I realise how profound is my love.'

Her breath beside his ear imparted a warm tingle:

'Auguste's farewell was forever, but we will be re-united, Friedrich. Believe it. We will. We will!'

A shift back to sanity came from someone unexpected. Georg Hegel arrived in Jena. An old face. A rational mind.

In their teen years Friedrich and Hegel had a kind of partnership against the arbitrary punishments meted out at Tübinger seminary. Now, at Friedrich's encouragement, and funded by an inheritance, Hegel secured a *privatdozent*, or unsalaried position, as lecturer at the university.

He had a powerful stare, as if he were reading and processing a range of information about the person being stared at. Friedrich wasn't intimidated by the man because they had been school friends, yet he could discern some newly-cultivated perception, perhaps a sharpening of Hegel's mental faculties. As if to highlight this awareness, the bags under Georg's eyes were becoming more prominent, forming the lower halves of large circles completed by his brows, like wide lenses that would leave nothing unnoticed.

Was he to be a colleague or a competitor?

Goethe summed up Hegel's arrival:

'One of the brightest minds in German philosophy has been added to Jena's luminaries.'

Hegel knew Friedrich as a friend and collaborator, but his entry into the academic circle had something artful about it, like a pine marten entering the city under cover of darkness, seeking food. He was Friedrich's co-worker, but regarded Fritz Schlegel rather differently: his potential competitor for a lectureship.

'Have you read Fritz's book, *Lucinde*?'

'Yes, I have.'

'The suspicion seems to be that Lucinde is modelled on his wife, Dorothea.'

'So I understand,' said Friedrich.

'Meaning it's a bildungsroman ... autobiographical.'

'I imagine so.'

'It seems to advocate a union of physical and spiritual love.'

'Which is ... unethical?'

'Well —'

'Why do you ask, Georg?'

'It's ... nothing.'

An impending contest between Georg Hegel and Fritz Schlegel? If so, Friedrich had no interest in feeding it. There was already enough antagonism — between the Schlegel brothers, Caroline and Dorothea, between the good citizens of Jena and the militarist First

Consul of France, Napoleon. Change was in the air, like wind before a cloud-bank.

⁓

A gale swept in from the Gleisburg hills, declaring itself with hollow moans in the chimneys, followed by flurries of sleet. Friedrich could also hear another sound in the wind — the mournful *gordle-ordle-oo* of collared doves, huddling for shelter under the eaves outside his window.

Next to the fire, warm in his lodgings just outside Jena's walls, Friedrich continued his notes on art, finding himself recalling conversations with Novalis.

'To write, I need to be electrified,' said the poet.

'And where do you get this kind of excitement?'

'From others. From you, Fichte, Fritz, Caroline and August. New ideas, a changed viewpoint. Then I can enter the sunlit uplands of thought.'

'How much can poetry inform philosophy?'

'That's an interesting one, Friedrich. Just as a mathematical solution is elegant, so should a proposition in philosophy be poetic.'

Friedrich found himself stoking the fire with a smoking stick. And how am I to achieve that neat marriage of disciplines, unless — I can also become electrified?

The mail arrived just ten minutes later. It brought a letter from Caroline.

> *My dearest Friedrich,*
> *As if my sweet daughter were not enough, it seems death is moving in on another of our cherished hearts: Novalis.*

As I write, Fritz is at his bedside in Wiesenfels. He rushed there from Jena with the earnest wish he would not be too late. In the letter we received, Fritz wrote of his horror at how frail and vapid was his dear friend's appearance, against the inner one's approach to the final threshold.

August-Wilhelm keeps reassuring me, and he's right, that Novalis has a long-nurtured desire for the realm beyond death — a dark legacy of his period of melancholy, desperate to be re-united with Sophie. That's no reassurance for us. I fear we must prepare for life without him.

You will remember he expressed the strongest disapproval of our relationship, a sudden moralistic turn we couldn't understand. It is unfortunate we can't mend this rift with the past at such a crucial stage of his life.

Novalis, dead at only twenty-nine! Now there would be no answers to Friedrich's questions on philosophy, poetry, religion, art and science — at least, those coming from this unique, much loved artist. The contrast was stark: the poet electrified/the poet lifeless. Was the reverie of replayed conversation a premonition of what Caroline's letter had confirmed? It was impossible to know. Now there was only one certainty: Novalis was gone.

He could be more composed about it after the emotional upheaval of Auguste's death, but needed to examine his reactions. What had Novalis said? That death is night? Now he had slipped into it, a new star among timeless constellations.

Still, Friedrich wanted to ask the poet: Tell me how it ends. But there was an impenetrable barrier between the two of them. Suddenly, the space once occupied by the living and breathing poet was a vacuum. Wheels of the great chronological machine would wind inexorably onwards, while the short life of Novalis, finite, completed, receded into the past. Of all the memories they associated with him — his smiling face, the pensive look that was all his own, the ardent discussions they shared, his close, wide-eyed attentiveness — many would fade, but his poetry would remain as vital as ever.

There was also Novalis's passionate stand against the mechanised world science had been creating. He saw no poetry in formulae, categorisation, statistics, analysis and other rigid controls. Where was the ever-changing and unclassifiable side of life: nature, feeling, art and the depth dimension?

※

Caroline returned to Jena. It had been a year since she had left with Auguste. The homecoming felt strange.

The house had been rifled by Fritz and Dorothea and was in a deplorable state. Furniture, cookware and bedding had been pilfered and crockery chipped or smashed. She contacted them, but only caused acrimony. After some time Fritz grudgingly returned a few chattels, then severed all contact.

Friedrich returned to Leutragasse regularly for meals with Caroline, but they were forbidden to cohabit. He was well aware of the reasons, they were in his mind every day. In the eyes of the orthodox he was already trespassing on the sanctity of marriage. There were enough watchdogs in Jena to ensure protocol was maintained, and more attention than usual was paid to the headquarters of the Jena circle. She bought him a coat — at least he was able to wrap himself in her love.

But the coat couldn't shut out university politics: a sudden eruption between Friedrich and the hot-headed Fichte. Fichte had managed to revive his career, but was now vehemently denouncing Friedrich's *Naturphilosophie*.

'He's vindictive and unprofessional,' Caroline declared. 'You have to retaliate.'

'I will. Though it seems petty just to call him a liar.'

'Only strong language will work. Isn't that what he deserves?'

'There's a new development. Fichte is implying I'm just a hireling working for his grand plan.'

'How absurd,' said Caroline. 'He was lecturing before you, and probably can't lose the notion that, being younger, you're a subordinate. One of his lackeys.'

'It's expected philosophers will disagree with each other. It's the nature of the game.'

'You're being too generous, Friedrich.'

'But, I agree, we've got to preserve mutual respect.'

'Especially when he's implying that your ideas are a subset of his own. In Fichte's case it's all about triumphalism and hubris.'

The next day, Fichte burst into Friedrich's office, his face the colour of hot coal.

'These are not the ramblings of a self-centred pedant, as your students have parroted, but someone with whom you're unfamiliar: a logician!'

The outburst came with a scattershot of spittle.

'It's inevitable we'll have differences of opinion,' said Friedrich evenly. 'We're philosophers. But it's presumptuous to assert my theories stand only by virtue of your own.'

'My idealism of the I is a raptor hurled at sparrows!' exclaimed Fichte. "It has become the dominant school of thought, not just at this university, but across Germany!'

He puffed out his chest, then performed a pirouette as he turned for a quick exit, ensuring he had the last say.

Friedrich pictured the dispute with Fichte not as one of words and ideas but as a real physical brawl. He imagined the pugnacious philosopher squaring up with bare fists, rushing at him, knocking him down, then aiming punches at his face.

Would Friedrich fight back? Of course he would. Fichte may have had boldness and fury on his side, but Friedrich had youth. And wasn't this the nub of the issue? Fichte, twenty years older, was more hardened in his attitudes, while Friedrich had a different, fresher energy, which would ultimately prevail.

There was no question the man's bullish manner was partly responsible for the altercation. But there was another factor. Fichte was making the same mistake as Descartes, and needed correction: thinking is not only *my* thinking, just as existence is not only *my* existence. Friedrich's philosophy replaced the I with the Absolute. 'It thinks in me' was the keynote, ego becoming irrelevant.

'That dispute became rather dirty,' said Caroline after he had described the altercation. 'You'll need deep cleansing in a hot bath.'

⁓

Against the wrangle with Fichte, it was good to have a collaborator: Georg Hegel — even if their newly-conceived Disputorium seemed not to resolve disputes but promote them. Located in a building near the Natural History Society, it was set up like a court of law. But instead of felons being on trial, it was systems of thought and those who proposed them.

Hegel was not a good communicator, but this was no reflection on his insight and logical mind. Friedrich had long been interested in philosophical architecture, finding flaws in edifices of theory.

Would his taking on Hegel in this court of contested ideas be tantamount to a kind of status game? Friedrich's standing was high, and with foreign students arriving in Jena to attend his lectures, rising even higher. They often saw him take a scalpel to the extraneous gristle in the meat of his colleague's theories. Now the room was abuzz with the much anticipated match between the two philosophers.

Facing each other in the Disputorium, their audience ready for the clash, the issue of contention was announced by an ancient tutor with a bald pate, long earlobes and bushy eyebrows:

'An examination of Hegel's view that teaching philosophy is like teaching geometry.'

'In what way are these two disciplines the same?' asked Friedrich.

'In order to communicate, both require a regular structure.'

'About geometry I would agree, but with philosophy that is too prescriptive.'

'Why should they be any different?' asked Hegel, biting his lip in concentration. 'Both require exactitude and a predictable framework.'

'But philosophy is not so hidebound, or shouldn't be. It is informed by art and nature, neither of which can be plotted on a graph, nor have their angles measured.'

Friedrich could feel the ripple of agreement from his student supporters. Parry, and thrust.

'You can't begin philosophy with speculation based on feelings or the unquantifiable,' said Hegel. 'Reasoned analysis is the only way to build a philosophical system.'

'I begin philosophy with the experience of wonder. But that doesn't mean I abandon reason when looking for answers.'

'You value intuition, Friedrich, a means of enquiry as incompatible with logic as oil is with water.'

'You should know in your attention to history, Georg, that intuition has been devalued for that very reason: logic can't get any purchase on it. And by being devalued, it has atrophied.'

The debate continued into the night. Oil lamps were lit. In their flickering light, audience stalwarts remaining listened to the opposed voices reverberating around the *Disputorium's* wood-panelled walls.

⁓

Caroline and Friedrich were now on their own and intent on a divorce settlement with Schlegel, which would allow them to marry. Friedrich thought of Novalis: surely now the great Romantic would bless their union? An ally in this process was Goethe — judicious, generous, famous — able to exert pressure on the league of high-ranking officials in Weimar who would deliver the verdict on the case.

Schlegel, already decamped to Berlin, had another lover. To strain their crumbling marriage further, Caroline was demanding he pay a number of her outstanding debts. This stoked his anger. If a divorce could finally be authorised, both parties would be free to live their own lives. The process seemed painfully slow, until Caroline finally received a letter.

Friedrich looked over her shoulder as Caroline broke open the impressive-looking seal. His eyes skittered over the formalities, legalese and numbered points that filled the page, alighting on the one important message: divorce had been approved.

In candlelight, Friedrich watched as his hand clasped Caroline's, sealing that long-held promise in their palms. Their rings, nearly touching, reflected the gleam of the same flame.

Friedrich and Caroline Schelling, husband and wife, left Jena and moved to Würzburg. There was something uniquely artistic, playful and prosperous about the place, all expressed in one building: the little käppele on a hill, lovingly presiding over the city with its exuberant architecture of cupolas and roof lanterns.

Friedrich had taken up a lucrative post. At one of their first social events, Caroline met the university Chancellor who remarked:

'We really are proud to have Germany's most prominent philosopher on our staff.'

'I'm proud to have him in my bed,' was the rejoinder she kept to herself.

A large number of Friedrich's students had followed him. Now, in many ways, he could feel his life beginning. Caroline had the means to redress the disappointment of returning to her ransacked house in Jena. She was able to start again, buying new chairs, sofas and curtains, books, clothing, and the best food available for their cook. She was long past the role of gregarious hostess coping with a dozen guests, having found the good life instead.

After three years came another move, to Munich, where Friedrich had been offered a position at the city's Academy of Sciences. He was in his new office when a letter arrived from Hegel:

> *You may have heard of recent French conquests. Now they include Jena. Napoleon's troops have burned large parts of the town, the rest pillaged of anything that might feed or enrich the invaders. Before all this mayhem I had been struggling to complete my* Phenomenology of Spirit. *It was only by*

a miracle I could get the completed documents onto a mail coach that was neither commandeered nor destroyed during the attack. This work is the start of my career, Friedrich...

From their carriage the Schellings took in the dark beauty of forested Bavarian hills. It reminded Friedrich of the coach trip they had taken together at night from Weimar to Jena — enclosed, side by side, hands clasped, feeling the warmth of the other without having to speak. On the move, Caroline felt the liberation of wanderlust, like a vagrant with no destination. If she was willingly lost, it didn't matter; she was with her husband.

Their carriage passed along the Ammersee, through Herrsching, then further south, the majestic ridges of the Alps rising before them. Caroline was dressed for the journey in what Friedrich said was an 'enterprising' outfit of striped cotton with vandyked edging and Brandenburg buttons, a shift from the now tired classical look to a romantic one. Her loosened hair was a deliberate affront to current rules of coiffure — but she had flair and originality, so of course she would act against the trend.

Though Caroline was twelve years his senior, she was made twelve years younger by the panache in her dress and bearing. It was an energy and gaiety somehow augmented by their standing in prosperous academia, and by the removal of tensions in her life — the overheated Schlegel household, the deaths of Auguste and Novalis. Time, and the love of Friedrich, had allowed her to overcome the complications and the losses.

Friedrich could also take some pleasure in men's (and women's) jealous looks. It only reinforced the truth of the matter: she's mine.

He loved the simplicity of it; a man with his wife, travelling through a forest.

Outside was a land with many dangers: violence, disease and war. But for now, at least, in this enclosed, gently rocking space, all was secure and guaranteed. He needed no-one but Caroline. They had invested so much in each other. He knew her mercurial mind and wanted to know more, but realised — happily — it would be a process lasting years: the gradual unfoldment of the other. Somehow, without consciously looking for her, he had found a *seelenfreund*, a soul-mate. It was a gift. Close engagement with her, in conversation, was like a pair of birds fluttering together. He could feel the tingling brush of her warm feathers.

Friedrich noticed that Caroline had been leaning forward for some time, watching random breezes ruffling waves on the lake and a small fishing boat keeping pace with them. He took her arm, then saw the strain on her face.

'What is it, my love?'

'I'm trying to concentrate on the Ammersee.'

'I don't understand. Are you not feeling well?'

'Just something I ate in Seefeld, I imagine.'

'Do you think we should stop?'

'No. Your parents will be expecting us.'

They did stop, about ten minutes later, where Caroline had to relieve herself. Friedrich thought of Auguste: surely Caroline couldn't have the same condition?

Before long her face had gone pallid and she was doubled over with the slicing pain of stomach cramps. When they arrived at his parents' house she was put to bed straight away and a doctor summoned. This time Friedrich was forearmed: he would allow opium to be administered, and nothing more. Was this the same attacker that had found Auguste — invisible, deadly, but also, in Novalis's terms, an agency for reuniting mother and daughter?

He sat faithfully at her bedside, helping her to glasses of water and trying to cool her brow, when a wave of fever rose through her. He used words as medical weapons that might, for them both, repulse despondency.

'Are the pains any less now?'

'A little,' she sighed, her smile a brave attempt to reassure him, to affirm her usual manner.

'Your water jug is full, straight from last night's rain.'

'You're adorable,' she said, followed by a wince she couldn't hide.

'The doctor will come again soon.'

'Take my hand. There, that's it.'

It was warm and still. Their window open to the air, at first they heard the sound of a horse clup-clopping slowly along the pathway below, then a raven's croak.

Caroline took a deep breath, as though all her concentration had moved to their palms, warmly pressed together. Looking into Friedrich's eyes, she said:

'Haven't we had such a wonderful life together?'

A smile rose up and bloomed across her face, just as his tears welled in response. She said:

'I've seen your career advance, always upward . . . and your brilliant mind . . .'

Caroline's face seemed to mist over, as if cloud had moved onto the high land where she'd placed them, and now she couldn't find him. She sighed, the pressure released from his hand, looking as if she had lapsed into sleep.

Was her fever returning?

Intimate conversation at her bedside did little to reassure him. Despite their love and care for each other, there were only flickers of their previous connection.

He asked her if the pains were less, but knew she was downplaying their effect on her. 'A little' could be masking any number of other feelings, like *lebensmüde*, life-tiredness, or fear.

He didn't want her to face this alone, but in the strict sense there was no way to complete mutuality. Another's thoughts were impenetrable. He could never unravel the mind of his beloved, and as much as he told himself their souls were one, he was unable to ever live from where she was living.

The feeling of her impending death was hard enough to bear, but behind it was a whole condition — the ground of sadness he had already tried to account for. His life experiences supplied other cases of sorrow: the zeitgeist of the Jena circle that had faded and was finished; the passing of the irreplaceable little Auguste; then of Novalis, the poet; news of Napoleon's troops occupying Jena, and of Hegel being forced to leave; then Würzburg falling to Austria during his next professorship there. The world was lurching from one conflict to another. And now his dear Caroline's decline. Nothing could stop it.

He thought of her desire for travel, the vital impulse in her, irresistible to others, too strong for them to curb. A world without Caroline was impossible. Caroline: the perfect fusion of intelligence, loving-kindness and verve. As long as she was still on this side . . .

He kept the channel open, his hand on hers, her words weakly reaching through to him, her eyes dwelling on his. Then they closed, and she was gone.

> *The region greatly upheaved itself; over it hovered my un-*
> *bound, newborn spirit.*
> *The mound became a cloud of dust, and through the cloud*
> *I saw the glorified face*
> *of my beloved. In her eyes eternity reposed. I laid hold of*
> *her hands, and the tears*
> *became a sparkling bond that could not be broken. Into the*
> *distance swept by, like*
> *a tempest, thousands of years. On her neck I welcomed*
> *new life with ecstatic tears.*
> *Never was such another dream; then first and ever since I*
> *hold fast an eternal,*
> *unchangeable faith in the heaven of the Night, and its*
> *Light, the Beloved.*

Novalis's *Hymn of the Night* couldn't be more real to him than at this time. Auguste's death had only been a rehearsal for confrontation with 'the night' and its near-irresistible pull, by his beloved, of every fibre in his body. The absoluteness of her sudden departure defied the richness, the meticulously-assembled intricacy, of her life.

'It's part of philosophy,' Friedrich once commented to Hegel. 'We strive for a reconciliation of opposites.'

The hardest opposition to reconcile at this juncture was, on the one side, the power of the All, a constant source of wonder, and on the other, that his loved one, at only forty-six, crowned with roses and daphne laureola, had been sent to her grave.

Friedrich, waiting in the wings before entry to the lectern, was now an imposing old gentleman of sixty-six, with a full head of white hair covering his ears, eyes of rinsed blue — penetrating, enquiring. A strong lower lip somehow conveyed self-possession and authority. How did these features of his physiognomy reflect the structure of the mind within? How could he sum up his now silent opponents, especially in front of those still alive and firmly in Hegel's camp?

As he stood in the shadows backstage, Friedrich cast back over a cavalcade of years peopled by colleagues, opponents, loved ones, kindred souls. He had outlived them all, but in his memory they were never completed. Each had a unique perspective on the world. So now, about to be welcomed onto the stage, how could he do justice to the thinkers he had encountered during his life? Being dead, his adversaries had no right of reply. But all had tested Friedrich's philosophy precisely because they, too, were brilliant minds.

Could they have been censured for passing over some *hintergedanke*, some underlying thought? This would be too harsh. He felt charitable to them all. Even Fichte. Flaws in their viewpoints or reasoning were not attacks on their personalities, but criticisms of how clearly they described the same reflection in the mirror of the self. All had scrutinised valleys of mental terrain and delved into its fissures — such was the driving force, and beauty, of contemplation.

Suddenly, they were announcing him.

'A long awaited return of the Meister Friedrich Schelling to the intellectual spotlight, exclusive to the University of Berlin. This man has conducted military engagements with Kant over dualism, with Fichte over subjective boundaries, and a battle royal with Hegel over rational boundaries.'

In spite of his age, Friedrich had lost none of his gravitas at the lecture. When his address was over there was, of course, a round of applause. Many of those present might have attempted to sum up, in one statement, Friedrich's lifelong journey into the mind. That statement could be gleaned from the Meister:

Man himself is that which is the most incomprehensible.

A Material Girl

D ARKNESS WAS COMING EARLY. Paris had just been drenched in an afternoon shower: a ceiling of cloud lingered. Leaving the smell of the Seine behind, a coach came splashing through the puddles on a street whose tall wooden buildings seemed to lean out over the cobbles. Vendors had disappeared during the rain, except for a man bent forward under the weight of firewood strapped to his back, his wares now sodden.

The fiacre — hired for short trips — clattered past him, turning right into Rue St Anthoine, past a stonemason's yard where an abandoned brazier still smoked after the dousing, then into the square of the Place Royale. A pair of footmen in mud-spattered boots and breeches were ready at the entrance of a building, one opening the door of the carriage for its sole occupant whose face was obscured by a cowl. Stepping onto the shiny cobbles, the passenger reached out, dropping two sous into the footman's hand.

Another carriage drew up to the same building. Three men emerged into a fixed lantern's yellowy glow. One, dressed in black, was Rene Descartes. Following him, wearing a cassock, was the Catholic priest, Pierre Gassendi, then the philosopher Thomas Hobbes, whose coat was damp, his ruff of hair in wet tendrils. They were ushered up a few short steps and through a door with thick iron hinges.

A few minutes later a third coach arrived, drawn by a pair of fastidiously caparisoned black horses, their manes and flanks glossy from the rain. This was an older vehicle, larger and more decorated than those that came before. A well-dressed postilion waited while a footman reached for the handle of a door framed in gilded ormolu inset with Venetian mirrors.

Cloud had further dimmed the city. The coach lantern caught a beading of raindrops on the glass as the door was swung wide. First, a gentleman emerged, then a young lady resplendent in satin, the silvery gown set off with a pearl necklace and earrings. On her head, a patrician's hat to guard her carefully-arranged hair from the rain. Most striking was her voluptuous body in thoroughly immoderate dress, chosen to convey just a hint of contempt for the more hidebound of the male company.

She followed her escort into a short, shadowy hallway adorned with stone pilasters rising either side of the tiled floor. On one side was a decorative plaque bearing various names. If she could read it in the gloom she would see no women were listed.

They continued into the main room. Her companion's body initially masked her from the men now seated around a circular oak table. Past him she saw Mersenne, whose cowl was drawn back over his shoulders, remark:

'I found the skies in Bordeaux strikingly clear, the better to observe the new moon.'

'It is fortunate the moon is an opaque reflector,' commented Descartes. 'Had it oceans, owls would be going hungry.'

The others laughed, more to ease the tension than in genuine amusement. A waiter used the moment to place a jug of wine on the table. Sir Charles Cavendish, acting as a protective wall between the sole female and this sequitur of logicians from the Academie Parisienne, spoke up.

'Forgive me, gentlemen. I have taken the liberty of inviting my sister-in-law to this meeting. Please accept her as a guest and . . . supporter of our investigations.'

He stepped aside. For a moment the candlelight dazzled her. She hoped they didn't notice the rush of blood to her cheeks.

'You're welcome, Madam,' said Mersenne, indicating a threadbare banquette off to the side, under a pair of leadlight-patterned windows, separated from the horseshoe of five chairs reserved for the men.

She found herself staring at her lap, where the V from the embroidered bodice joined the flare of her satin dress. Her hands, half-clasped in front of her, described the passivity and submission suitable to her role amongst these men. Her concentration had drifted to reminders of her inferior status, but now their voices came back into focus.

'Oh, I agree, Monsieur Descartes,' said Hobbes, 'that spirits are something. They have dimensions and thus, quite clearly, bodies.'

'But you misconstrue our mentality, a substance unique in nature and immediately verifiable by introspection.'

They will have assumed these lines of argument would be lost on a feeble feminine mind, that her presence at the meeting was primarily ornamental, an embellishment, like a vase of flowers, especially without her husband by her side. Mersenne's fraternity would need convincing that she was there for the same reason they were: to discuss philosophy.

Though mute, she was following, quite competently, the line of enquiry. They indulged her, this young marchioness called Margaret, known to some by the sobriquet, Mad Madge.

Now, she wanted to put her oar into the conversation, and the unvoiced line was ready:

'There may indeed be the immaterial things that you affirm, Monsieur Descartes. But how can we investigate the immaterial?'

She imagined her high-pitched, reedy voice suddenly overlaying the resonant, stentorian tones of the men. Would they deign to respond? The truth was that her silence was more due to natural reticence. She had to console herself that at least she was present at this philosophical circle, thanks to Thomas Hobbes' long acquaintance with her husband's family.

Then, the more personal, considered account of what followed:

I took a good draught of wine from the pewter goblet at my side table, stood, and moved closer to the window. Monsieur Mersenne noticed the brief rush of satin like silver reeds in a breeze, probably assuming I was a little cramped and needed to stretch. Mersenne, the polymath, priest of prime numbers, a prolific correspondent. They said he was in touch with a hundred philosophers, astronomers and mathematicians across Europe.

My heels' metronomic click on the floor supplied a brief, distracting tempo to the ongoing debate. The venerable Hobbes, his bald forehead and wrinkled face flanked by bushy grey curls, joined in again.

'There is nothing more to spirit than the physical movements described by science.'

Descartes was quick to respond.

'Our not understanding how physical bodies and immaterial minds interact is no confirmation that they don't interact.'

My approach to the crescent of chairs stifled any response to Descartes' statement. I arrived with an air of amour propre, and the advantage of height. Speaking as clearly as possible, I said:

'Nothing in a body's performance may be accounted for by an immaterial agent, whether God or a so-called disembodied spirit. Bodies have the wherewithal to perform everything by themselves.'

Pierre Gassendi seemed about to speak, but Descartes had the riposte:

'The idea of thinking matter makes no sense, so we can't hold that all reality is material.'

Hobbes could have entered the fray then, but he kept out. Having learned from his books I could offer my own support. I said:

'Even if we were to allow immaterial things in reality, we could neither perceive them nor have any concept of them.'

'And what of feeling and imagination,' said Descartes. 'These are immaterial, but we know very well what they are, because we imagine, and we feel.'

'Sensory information is the most reliable,' I said. 'Least reliable are unperceivable essences.'

Was the argument getting any more heated than before I spoke up? It seemed that the men started in civilised debate, and when I joined it became an altercation. I had entered as Gassendi's ideological ally: his eyes' darting exploration of my body in its watery shimmer showed one kind of appreciation. But there had been an infringement of protocol. Sparrow-brained women should never trespass on territories of science and philosophy patrolled exclusively by men. It challenged them. Then, if I gained any purchase on their arguments, which I believed I did, both my *youth and sex would further disarm them. That was my hope. Anything to avoid sly smiles at a woman's unguarded follies.*

There was no need to worry on these counts. The 'altercation' never happened, except in the pages of her diary. Knowing the men would not include her in debate, she had to imagine her own involvement instead, so went to her inkstand and quill. Only in this way could she put her enquiring mind to the test.

Returning from Mersenne's gathering, her resolve was hardening. She would pursue, herself, these issues aired in the meeting of men's minds. That it was both difficult and fascinating was the reason her metier had been unearthed: what could be more fulfilling than the life of the mind?

She enjoyed the serious game of rational argument, but also felt a creative power waiting inside like a sleek young mare, ready to break free of its halter and take off at full gallop.

~

Her husband often being out on business, Margaret would retreat to the bedroom, her only sanctuary in a small, all-male pied-à-terre, a place free from *the encumbered cares and vexations, troubles and perturbance of the world.*

She sat with her pen and paper in the same place, on the same chair upholstered in a soft leather secured with rows of domed brass studs. A clock set into a porcelain vase, clanking quietly on the bedside table, measured her thoughts as she considered how the last turbulent years might inspire her writing.

She remembered the stocktake on her life at age eighteen in Colchester. It seemed of no consequence, insulated from the real world, hampered further by a timidity she couldn't shake.

It all changed with a violent incursion.

Dinner table discussions concerned how English society had been riven by religious dissent, excessive taxation and disrupted trade. Margaret was staying at her sister's house when she had a premonition something was wrong.

The next day confirmed it. Her family home had been attacked by a mob of Roundheads. How could they believe this isolated family, loyal to King and Church, was somehow directly responsible for their grievances? The mob stormed the house, ransacking every room for valuables and hauling off her mother Elizabeth, her brother John, and his wife. John later told Margaret:

'Were it not for the guards escorting us to jail, the inflamed crowd would likely have battered us to death.'

She found it hard to credit such vitriol and the vandalism that resulted; from far and wide people came, joining in the rampage, wrecking the Lucas house, looting it for live fowl, preserves, cereals, silks, bed-linen, dresses, tapestries and plate, then smashing their family tombs in the nearby churchyard and throwing rocks through the stained glass windows.

When her dispossessed family reunited in Oxford, Margaret's only thoughts were of escape. She could find escape in her writing, but the immediate priority was finding some refuge from violence and disorder.

The stars were aligned, though in no hurry to exert their influence.

Queen Henrietta arrived in Oxford after almost perishing in a storm at sea, then eluding a gang of rebels. Married to Charles I, but never crowned due to her Roman Catholicism, she had strong ideas about how to fight Parliamentary insurgents opposed to the monarchy, and how to make best use of her power.

Margaret was in the front row of spectators when she paraded through the streets like a conquering heroine. Hawkers seized the chance to sell produce. Cries of 'Fine mutton pies,' 'Milk straight from the udder' and 'Oysters pale and shining' competed with the hubbub of an excited crowd, the hawkers' barrows forcing bystanders onto the road so that Henrietta's coach was all but halted by the throng, causing one horse to stamp its shoes on the cobbles in annoyance.

For Margaret the event had just the right degree of danger, the romance of it also appealing to her, as it did to others in the crowd.

'You'd never know she's beaten the North Sea gales.'

'Her triumph is ours, too.'

'And her gown looks perfect.'

'There's breeding for you.'

Was it true — the rumour that the queen was short of staff? She had to act quickly, knowing this move would work against her nature, exposing her. *Few doth live as they should, that is, to live within themselves.*

Could she, in all conscience, abandon her beleaguered family? Then if she were to seek a life at court, how to impress the Queen? If it was by confidence and verbal expressiveness, then she was sunk. So how to seize the opportunity?

Her brother John arranged a meeting at the Queen's chambers, Merton College. Margaret spent hours on how to present herself, what dress to wear, and what rehearsed lines would loosen a stilted encounter. What she hadn't foreseen was a place full of dogs, several barking and one rearing up, its paws scratching her flawless satin gown.

Henrietta, heavily pregnant, seemed oblivious to the feral welcome.

'Are you able to look after an infant?'

'I've helped my sister with her baby daughter.'

Did Henrietta see her blush? Did she read the lie that prompted it?

'Do you dress your own hair, Margaret?'

'Yes, I do.'

'It shows competence.'

'I would hope so, your highness.'

'Mitte!'

A woolly dog like a long-legged sheep came bounding up to the Queen, licking her hand with its slavering tongue.

'This is Mitte. Could you manage my pet?'

The dog turned to eye Margaret, as if waiting for the answer.

'I'll do whatever your highness requires.'

'You're very . . . reserved. Self-contained.'

She couldn't think of a response.

'Can you start straight away?'

Margaret was appointed the Queen's new Maid of Honour.

She entered the court. Posing and parading were dukes and duchesses, patricians and poodles, yeomen in hose of bright yellow, tall African men in white frock coats, mesomorphs strong enough to lift a lady on each arm, foul-mouthed soldiers, and flirting husband-seekers in costumes of furbelows and feathers.

Margaret had a unique standpoint on this drama — that everything arises from natural properties and causes, so bodies must be informing each other about comportment and connection: *Nature's parts move themselves, and are not moved by any agent. They are self-moving and self-knowing.*

It was during intimate times with the Queen — the rituals of dressing, bathing, fitting shoes, fixing the hair or simply waiting for her — that Margaret felt this natural reciprocity and negotiation between bodies. She once made the mistake of engaging the Queen about this subject.

'Do you have a picture of how your hair should be styled?'

'I leave that to you, Margaret.'

'And you find it acceptable, Your Highness?'

'Yes, I trust you. But you're talking in riddles. What is your point?'

'Pardon me, but preparing your hair is something we've never discussed. It's a transaction, or arrangement, between bodies. I seem to know how you would like to appear and . . . my hands produce it.'

That's when she dropped the hairbrush onto the floor, denting the handle but absolving her of any further explanation — and Henrietta of any further bewilderment. What she had read and absorbed from Thomas Hobbes was that, since everything is material, matter thinks. Anything understood, defined, pondered or confronted, is material.

Margaret might have had dominion over the Queen's hair, but the Queen had dominion over her maid's body.

―

It didn't take much for Margaret to recognise the reasons the Queen should flee the country. She wouldn't give an inch to the Parliamentarians, so they brought a charge of treason against her, then wrecked a Rubens altarpiece in her private chapel.

Henrietta and her diminished retinue took the road to Bath, the King accompanying her, Margaret fearful her mistress, close to giving birth, might be caught and arrested at any time. They continued, without the King, to Exeter, the Earl of Essex in pursuit.

'What will show itself first?' asked the Queen, distraught, as Margaret mopped her brow. 'Essex from without, or my baby from within?'

Even when Princess Henrietta came into the world, there wasn't a moment to lose. If captured, the Queen would give Essex leverage over Charles I. France was the only option left. The newborn had to be abandoned. Margaret would never forget the sight of baby Henrietta in swaddling clothes, her little fists punching the air, as if it held the faces of her mother's enemies.

Her child lost and a fugitive from her own country, the Queen was inconsolable.

Margaret knew only too well the perils of sea travel, though she had never ventured from shore. But duty to the Queen had to override these qualms. They boarded a galley in Falmouth and set sail for France. Margaret was unnerved at the creaking of timbers, feeling the merciless power of waves directed down the channel against them, and imagining too easily their vessel breaking apart under the strain: splintering, then the sea flooding in to swamp them all and drive them under.

She would rather flay her skin with hair cloth than sail, but Henrietta was sanguine about it; she had done this before and expected a safe delivery onto French soil. Margaret had no such expectation. They had set to sea in a hull of caulked wood — any change in the weather or mismanagement by the crew could spell disaster. It would be an early death. The thought that her literary life would go unlived filled her with dread. It didn't help that Henrietta's other maids were callow landlubbers like herself. Mere minutes out from shore all were staggering against the pitching floor: one was turning green.

Never had the English Channel seemed so wide. Below deck

Margaret used all her willpower to maintain poise and control against the body's mounting nausea, her stomach in tune with the vessel's pitching and yawing in heavy seas. There was nothing to stop the uprising. Margaret and the ladies-in-waiting spewed into the bilges. But a bigger drama was occurring outside. There was a crash as a cannon-ball hit the rigging, splintering timbers and severing ropes. She was terrified. *My hands shook as if I had the palsy.* They had been ambushed by the Parliamentarian's warships.

'Row for your lives,' she heard Henrietta call. Oarsmen were their only hope of not being sunk or captured, but from below deck Margaret — dizzy and disoriented — could imagine their pursuers gaining on them. The seas grew heavier; a strong wind made shouts from the deck inaudible. She knew this was how ships went down, the way passengers drowned. Under a second wave of nausea she pictured the imminent possibility of being obliterated by a second cannon ball, cast into the sea or blown off course. But the rowers were steadfast, powering them into the lee of land. It was Brest. They had landed in France.

Margaret didn't mind the long journey across a landscape roasting in the summer sun. It was solid earth. With no imminent danger she didn't mind ministering to a troubled Queen sobbing for her child on the other side of the channel.

Henrietta had the delicacy and grace Margaret expected of a Queen. Yet other qualities came to the fore or went into abeyance depending on the people and places surrounding her. There was the determination and sense of purpose she had seen when Henrietta paraded down the streets of Oxford, and there was a melancholy both profound and beautiful that cooled her whole demeanour and expression into a forlorn, unfathomable look. Margaret thought it her duty to recognise these different tempers in the Queen, to foster her resolve and willpower while reversing any lapse into dejection. Could she do this? Or had these frames of mind become too much a part of Henrietta's constitution?

They arrived in Paris: the buildings majestic, the streets teeming, the smell unignorable. Margaret was prescribed laudanum to deal with the shock.

The scale of the city and its crowds was overwhelming. One of Margaret's duties was to ensure the Queen's drinking water came from springs outside the city and not from the heavily-polluted Seine. She had much to learn. For the odd occasion she needed to venture out into the streets, warnings were given about gangs of thieves who trained children to feign rabies or blindness for coins. Others were adept at slicing the straps holding prosperous Parisians' purses, then fleeing with their prize into the maze of streets so spread with mud, rubbish and horse-droppings as to sully any pair of fine shoes that attempted pursuit.

She kept well clear of heavy wooden signs overhead — boulangerie, cordonnier, boucher — in the cramped and crooked streets, lest their frayed ropes broke and flattened her. Her shortcut to the Seine took her through jostling crowds, fruit sellers in full cry and imploring beggar-children. Dog-eared leaflets for theatre productions were pasted in repeater patterns across wooden walls. A lady with a high-crested wig passed by, seated in a litter and holding a tiny dog with bulbous eyes. It was the city's great parade of humanity: fascinating but foreign.

Once she came upon a grand procession of the city's ecclesiastical hierarchy. The Archbishop was leading, barefooted and in canonical robes. Behind this colourful figure were ranks of monks in grey cassocks, then nuns slipping silently past in funereal black. Another group in priestly vesture had caskets of relics borne aloft on a catafalque, as though the sombre cortège was to end with their burial.

Margaret shivered and turned away. It seemed that Paris had engulfed her, the columns of clergy not about piety but mourning.

For some, the court was a kingdom of sensuality: fine food, wine, amorous games between available women and sportive suitors. But it was also a place where men must endeavour to get wives before they were encloistered.

Margaret had hoped for a more refined life, of the comme il faut — exemplary etiquette and deportment, educated discussion and bonhomie. She found this, but it was tempered with spite, double-dealing and promiscuity. She witnessed an ignoble, dissolute breed of ladies who lounged immodestly, flaunted themselves with lubricious looks, and fell into men's arms at any opportunity. She once spotted a shameless rake suckling a woman's proffered breast behind a pillar. Gossip spread like the pox; all had to be vigilant for lies and deceptions. As Margaret learned: *When whispers start, barricade your ears.*

Matrimony was an escape route from this intense, crowded life. For a lady not already promised to someone, court was an open market. Eligible young bachelors were rare, but a man of means might drift into their orbit.

Such as the bon vivant, William Cavendish. He offered an opportunity.

Court tittle-tattle revealed that William had married thirty years before, his wife dying young, but bearing him two sons and two daughters. As a military commander, what little innate skill he brought to the battlefield was well compensated by courage, loyalty and many years experience in horsemanship. Away from the clash of swords and blasts of cannon-fire he was known as a patron of the arts. He was also a ladies' man and connoisseur of the good life, a gallant who liked to lay siege to the affections of attractive women with verses both tender and erotic.

When he first visited Queen Henrietta's court, Margaret and the other ladies saw a mature but still attractive gentleman in a dark coat like a cape with matching vest and breeches. He displayed the elegance typical of aristocratic fashion, the hem of his sleeves folded back, creating a wide cuff embellished with lace. Bows on shoes and garters and a cutlass at his side completed the picture of a wealthy, influential royalist.

The ladies-in-waiting tried their best to be noticed. It would take just the right mix of youth, sartorial flair and natural beauty to catch his eye. And the chances were slight: he might only visit once, making just one sweep of his gaze across the bevy of eligible women. Margaret felt gauche, an ingénue, that if she opened her mouth she was sure to utter a faux pas. To her competitors, if that's what they were, the prim, tight-lipped Margaret Lucas would be the last of them on whom he would focus attention.

They were wrong.

Something of her beauty and reserve attracted him instantly. Perhaps it was her understatement, or he could discern an intelligence the other contenders lacked.

Only his eyes were fixed upon her, nor had he power to speak; and she perceiving where he was, for her eye had secretly hunted him out, would as often look upon him as her modesty would give her leave. She knew in her heart that William would be the love of her life.

Their wooing, conducted at first through ardent verses carried by messengers, was not missed by the more observant women at court. The love letters delivered, how could she know the couriers weren't stopping en route to read, perhaps memorise, their lyrics of love, smelling the lavender in which hers were steeped? Secrets kept from the Queen were considered lèse majesté, and could have serious consequences, but Margaret saw her chance for escape. It couldn't come fast enough. She had to use all her forbearance and self-control to weather the jealous looks, the bitter humour overheard: our Illustrious Guardian of Morality, Marge the Maiden of Modesty, and Little Miss Frigid.

But every new letter and its words of affection built more promise, more certainty, that William's amorous intentions would be sealed by marriage. Truly, lovingly, kindly, his words had somehow found and defined a hitherto untouched territory in her mind — the rising topography of her future life. Already she felt new ideas germinating in its richer earth.

On one of the rare but precious times they were alone, Margaret spoke with candour and assurance:

'You must know your verses have captured my heart. But there's more.'

'More joy, dear Margaret?'

'They have kindled an expressiveness in my writing.'

'Then I'm doubly happy.'

'I feel you inspired that image you read yesterday in my letter: *I know my small bark will swim the better and safer for your steerage*.'

'Ah, yes. So you had no fear to launch it into the deepest waters.'

'Exactly.'

'We can navigate this dangerous world together.'

Margaret could hardly credit her good fortune. In times of solitude, fears would steal in that the Marquess William Cavendish was just a mountebank scouring Parisian salons for gullible young women, charming them with blandishments, his only objective the bed-chamber. Why else would he set his eyes on the retiring Margaret Lucas?

But fears were only natural — to safeguard her own future, her own security. She also had reasons for confidence: the mark of authenticity wasn't just his tunnel vision toward her and avoidance of the other attractive (and gregarious) women, it was a sincerity in his verse that could not be faked. Yes, she would step into that small bark with him, and head to the horizon.

They were married in a private ceremony on a day of crisp autumn sunshine. The Marquess Cavendish and his young Marchioness were too distinguished-looking for the small church: William, mighty, handsome and dashing in his military regalia, Margaret glorious in the aqueous sheen of a satin gown, cerise powder pinking the natural pallor of her cheeks.

She knew it was the beginning of a great adventure: *Her delights are the compass by which she sails, her love is his voyage, her advice his oracle; and doing this, he doth honour to himself by setting a considerable value on what is his own.*

Margaret knew her husband was a royalist, and that like her he was in exile. Separated from his estates, she guessed early in their courtship that the landed elite had fallen, that the wealth into which both had been born now meant very little. Consideration for his wife's happiness led William to avoid talk of money. He wanted to insulate her from the reality of constant borrowings that propped up their lifestyle.

But after Margaret's cautious enquiry he did confide in her about his part in the Civil War, which led to his exile.

'My brother Thomas said that in York you were known as a loyal hero.'

'That's kind of him,' said William, pouring himself a glass of brandy.

'Marston Moor?'

'It was the showdown. Prince Rupert had a battle plan I found unconvincing, but I was outranked. Added to this, we faced an uphill battle. I'm sorry, my love, should I go on?' he asked, turning his glass in circles to swirl the spirits. 'Women usually find such details distressing.'

He was ready to sidestep various images that rose in his mind: his soldiers singing psalms before battle then being targets of an artillery barrage, sudden explosions of mortar shells, bodies blown to bits, and of being a commander dealing with disease and desertions.

Margaret replied: 'You're here in Paris, and alive, for which I'm profoundly grateful. I'll never tire of learning about your life.'

'Very well,' he nodded, taking a drink.

Calling to mind the theatre of Marston Moor, William became an actor on a stage, as dramatic as Shakespeare's Henry V before Harfleur. His re-living of the trials and intensity of battle compelled him to make wide gestures, to clench his fists, and pace with the frustration of lost time not used to good effect.

'Cromwell and Lord Fairfax's cavalry were greater in number than our own, and arrayed on the high ground.' He stopped, sighed and shook his head. 'What sacrifices we made on that day, Margaret. We were overrun. By nightfall two thirds of my royalist forces were dead, wounded or captured.'

She saw him despair at the blood spilled, the human losses, dropping his arms and shaking his head.

He was right. One part of her did want to learn of his past life, to join in the imagery he had created, his rallying of the troops. But she also abhorred violence and human suffering. Was a more civilised and peaceful future too much to hope for?

'Thomas said you fought to the last.'

'But we had lost north-east England to the Parliamentarians and Covenanters. I remember seeing Lord Fairfax's breastplate shining in a ray of sun through the cloud, the victor consecrated from the heavens.' He savoured another sip of brandy. 'I've since asked myself: Was escape the only course left to me?'

'It boils down to one thing,' said Margaret. 'What was the honourable course of action?'

'I remember looking out at a moor soaked in the blood of royalist soldiers,' William continued. 'There were three paths ahead of me. I could surrender to Cromwell and Fairfax, escape to the continent, or die. With exile came loss of my standing and authority in England, loss of wealth and self-respect. But the alternative was to bow down in submission to the true traitors — of the monarchy.'

England had become a dangerous foreign land. Margaret's family was trapped there and becoming increasingly exposed. That Margaret lacked a dowry was of no concern to her husband. Thirty years her senior, William became the centre of her life. She saw his seniority as an asset: *Let me tell you, that what beauty and favour Time takes from the body, he gives double proportions of knowledge and understanding to the mind.*

She had someone who appreciated her intelligence and shared her interests in music, literature and the theatre. By marriage, she had affirmed her place in the English aristocracy. Now there was just the issue of their exile, straitened circumstances, and having to share a small house near the Louvre with Sir Charles, William's two sons from his first marriage, and various staff.

'It saddens me,' said Margaret, 'that we can barely graze two sous together.'

'Think nothing of it. We're partners in penury.'

'I dearly wish to help.'

'You have.'

'The bijoux and trumpery I've sold for cash? Just enough for a day's prosperity.'

'Remember, your mother has helped us,' said William.

'She's a wise accountant. All credit to her I've avoided pawning my dresses.'

'We're not destitute yet, my love.'

'If we were, I still wouldn't pawn my dresses.'

'Angels must be obeyed.'

Margaret had high ambitions. Knowing that nothing is difficult to a willing mind, she was to be not just a writer but *a meteor of the time*. In a man's world *she would shoot forth words like bullets with the fire of anger*. Her noble lord and husband would show the authority and bravery tested in battle to publish his wife's work at a time when no woman would dare publish.

Her reticence in front of others was counterbalanced in private by a recklessness with her pen; her lack of education countered by a trust in her own ability. Using the written word, she would stride into the male world just as she had imagined herself doing, and had recorded in her diary, after Mersenne's meeting — confident, direct, her mind charged with wild ideas.

In keeping with the incendiary times, Margaret wrote *The Blazing World*. A work of imagination, she believed, would draw the mind away from more serious contemplations. She wanted to show other women, by example, the satisfaction to be gained by creating visionary worlds.

Fictions are an issue of man's fancy, framed in his own mind, according as he pleases, without regard whether the thing he fancies, be really existent without his mind or not, so that reason searches the depth of nature, and enquires after the true causes of natural effects, but fancy creates its own accord whatever it pleases, and delights in its own work.

Her story commenced with a young lady captivating an adventurous trader who took her to sea. Gales blew the vessel towards the North Pole, where the trader and seamen froze to death. But *the young lady, by the light of her beauty, the heat of her youth and protection of the gods, remained alive.*

She found a fantastic empire of talking animals, all willing to converse with this 'Empress' about the nature of reality. In this world, creatures *were not acquainted with foreign wars or home-bred insurrections.*

The lady was extremely stricken with fear, and could entertain no other thoughts, but that every moment of her life was to be a sacrifice to their cruelty; but these bear-like creatures how terrible soever they appeared to her sight yet they were so far from exercising any cruelty upon her, that rather they showed her all civility and kindness imaginable, for she not being able to go upon the ice, by reason of its slipperiness, they took her up in their rough arms, and carried her into their city.

By consulting with the bear-men, ant-men, geese-men, spider-men, lice-men, fox-men, ape-men, jackdaw-men and parrot-men, she built a world in which all physical, biological, aesthetic and ethical aspects of life could be re-examined. Using the Empress as a mouthpiece, Margaret showed how intensely curious she was about the world.

> *She asked further, whether human bodies were not burdensome to human souls. They answered that bodies made souls active, as giving them motion, and if action was troublesome to souls, then bodies were so too. She asked again, whether souls did choose bodies. They answered: the souls of lovers lived in the bodies of their beloved.*

The hybrid creatures of *The Blazing World* were Margaret's allies in all affairs of state and culture, just as William was the means of bringing them to the page. He supported its publication from start to finish, adding his own words in the preface:

> *Then what are You, having no chaos found*
> *To make a World, or any such least ground?*
> *But your creating Fancy, thought it fit*
> *To make your World of Nothing, but pure Wit.*
> *Your blazing-world, beyond the Stars mounts higher,*
> *Enlightens all with a Celestial Fire.*

Margaret was convinced her feminine perspective and fertile imagination could outfox a male mind hemmed-in by rationality. Certain of her ability, she was eager to put it to the test.

~

Thomas Hobbes was coming to dinner. Knowing his greater experience in philosophy, she hoped for an evening of stimulating conversation. Though Hobbes was committed to instructing the young Charles, Prince of Wales, her husband might persuade the old philosopher to consider his wife as well — an appeal to noblesse oblige.

Some gentle persuasion in William's direction led to Hobbes accepting the invitation. The men had had a long association, touring Europe together in their youth. This earlier William had a rakish look, his dark moustache and beard trimmed to points, suggesting a figure somewhere between an elegant French fencer and a magician. Though he was now greying and a little gaunt, the stylish name would never change: *Cavendish* had the ring of audacity, or savagery. Outlandish, devilish, it suggested these, but was neither.

So there was something distinguished and different in the name Margaret had gained through marriage just two years before. William was her *grande passion*, her opportunity for transformation.

On the evening of the dinner she stood in the oval of a cheval mirror, looking for the right mix of the aesthetic and the agreeable: her chosen dress had a light blue moiré fabric, slashed sleeves showing folds of an orange under-skin. It was this detail, along with the half-mask of rouged cheeks and lips, the pencilled brows, and tumbling helices of hair, that presented a deliberate, enhanced version of herself.

Clothing and make-up could be a charming veil cast over the body, partly obscuring the inner. Orange under the sleeve gave this hint of the hidden, a fiery colour in love with its cool opposite. Aside from the attire, what was inside and bore her name sometimes felt disembodied, even ghostly. But she was averse to admit anything of Descartes' metaphysics. Margaret took pleasure in modifying her materiality instead:

I'll clothe myself with softest silk, and linen fine and white as milk.

The result, she believed, was copied by the glass. It took on her image by some matching process: an act of accord. So as she averted her eyes, then turned back to the mirror with a look of coolness and dignity, this hauteur was figured out immediately and returned. The image was refined, aristocratic, reflective of her correct place in society. She was ready to present this picture to Hobbes and her husband.

But first, she turned to the other glass, a window of nine small panes giving onto Rue Honnoré, one of the cleaner and wider streets in Paris, spared the usual mèlée of wagons, waifs, cattle, carts, pedlars and beggars. The last of the evening's sun in late April slanted golden onto a church façade. She could see an oil lantern being lit.

A carriage clattered around the paving stones, coming to rest under the window. The horse shook its head, jangling its metalwork, then the door was opened and there was Thomas Hobbes in a brown coat and new breeches. He didn't know how much she had learned from his *Meditations*. But was he even interested in her own ideas? She would soon find out. He knew nothing, and she would never tell him, of the foreign philosophers she had consulted in *The Blazing World*, then the different animals with their specialities in astronomy, chemistry, logic, architecture and more. She had been carried aloft to the alpine heights of imagination, the discussions being ways to exercise and challenge her, but now she had to shift to a literal, formulaic frame of mind.

From her God's eye view, Hobbes's bald dome was catching the first rays of the glowing lantern.

She waited until William had received and welcomed their visitor, then descended, catching the aroma of cypress and juniper they had saved for the fire.

Dinner was poached salmon, quenelles, croquettes with cream, dried figs, cheeses and jam tarts. Margaret was pleased the light had been reduced to just two candle sconces on one wall, and a triple-flame girandole next to a flask of wine in the centre of the table. She usually shunned alcohol, but this evening had an opportunity — she needed to loosen her tongue. And didn't they say wine may abate the vapours and pacify the spleen?

The setting was muted, restful, intimate. William opened the conversation.

'My dear Margaret tells me she was most pleasantly diverted at Monsieur Mersenne's salon.'

She had said nothing of the sort, but it was a suitably genial comment.

'I'm pleased to hear it,' replied Hobbes, cutting into a creamy croquette.

'I was interested to participate in some lines of enquiry,' she said.

Seeing that Hobbes' mouth was full, William continued on her behalf.

'Margaret told me of her brother John, a prominent scholar in law and philosophy, who assisted the development of her critical thought.'

'Most commendable,' Hobbes responded, quaffing his wine, crimson drips clinging to the ends of his moustache.

'May I ask,' she said, 'just as a matter of curiosity, if you would hold that only those things having dimension are real?'

He turned to regard her, his eyes just pinpricks of light in shadowed sockets.

'Yes,' he said, slowly, as though guarding an exposed inner sanctum.

'And I agree with you. But I'm not sure that every existent is material.'

No response. Was he waiting? She went on.

'Isn't it conceivable we could be encircled by immaterial things, yet are unable to perceive them?'

He sighed. During the reply he examined his wine goblet as if there were some flaw in the chased metal.

'Whatever is without dimension is not part of the universe. If spirits are taken to be real then they must have dimensions, or in other words, bodies.'

'Could it be possible though,' Margaret suggested, warming to the discussion, 'that a facet of our minds is immaterial, in order that it can recognise the immaterial?'

'No, that would be an exception to the rule,' he declared, spearing a quenelle with his fork and feeding it under the parted bush of his moustache.

'So how could anyone conceive of God, the ultimate immaterial, and how could they have faith?'

'Mmm, that meat is very well cooked,' said Hobbes, finding his escape route.

'Slaughtered just yesterday, so the kitchen staff tell me,' William added with a feigned smile.

The agenda of discussion had all been worked out in her mind: being a materialist, Hobbes must subscribe to the idea of a world made of atoms. But how could atoms be both designer and material? Surely they must be vitalised, knowledgeable, whether leaf, pebble, cat's whisker or rosebud? And then, how could such atoms team up without quarrelling?

She began to make another world, according to Hobbes's opinion, but when all the parts of this imaginary world came to press and drive each other, they seemed like a company of wolves that worry sheep, or like so many dogs that hunt after hares; and when she found a reaction equal to those pressures, her mind was so squeezed together that her thoughts could neither move forward nor backward, which caused such a horrible pain in her head.

Not wanting to discourage his wife from her chosen area of study, or show any disapproval, William said nothing of the air of tension at the table, or Hobbes' early departure. He did report, some days later, that their visitor had fallen ill. It seemed suspiciously convenient, given that Margaret wanted future meetings with Hobbes to burnish her critical faculties, and William was tasked with making this request to his friend.

Without Hobbes as an intellectual counterpart, and without his assisting her entry to Mersenne's forum of discussion, Margaret had difficulty engaging with other minds. It was a kind of ostracism.

For some of the young (and not so young) gallants at court, the greatest threat to future happiness was to marry an intelligent woman. One must shy away if she was articulate and informed. A wife must be attractive, supportive, obedient and ignorant. It will also be assumed that, through countless hours of practice, she is adept with a needle and thimble. This is her true vocation, the repetitive action keeping her weak wits occupied. When it comes to the life of the mind, any normal woman's conversation is no deeper than puddle water.

Margaret despaired at the silliness of her sex. She detested cheap romantic tales kept alive by women who fell for their oversweet sentiments and formulaic plots. She was more encouraged by the continental attitude than the English: in Paris she sensed that knowledge and intellect were valued for their own sake. An educated woman was not automatically barred from male society.

The way Margaret had been brought up, a woman from a family of means lived to eventually be auctioned off, hopefully to a man with the fattest purse and biggest assets. Then she would be sentenced to a superficial existence as a mere ornament on the arm of a man who was free to lead his authentic life.

It seemed a woman's lot was to be punished with a severe husband or tortured with a debauched one. But what puzzled her the most was why it should be so unacceptable that a man and woman might marry for love: *Women live like bats or owls, labour like beasts and die like worms.*

Still smarting from her failure to engage Hobbes at the dinner table, Margaret sought revenge in her diary:

> M: *I see no reason why a woman cannot join, as an equal, the man's world.*
>
> H: *It is because they fall short of reasoned judgement, impeding the progress of argument.*
>
> M: *Gender is but a physical distinction, implying nothing about differences in intellect.*
>
> H: *I still hold to my point that women are not equipped to rationalise.*
>
> M: *I suggest you take the time, Mr Hobbes, to consider how we are brought up. Even educated women from privileged backgrounds are expected to stay silent in male company, should any subject from science or philosophy be under discussion. The mistake you make is to link such conditioning with a substandard constitution.*
>
> H: *(Now irascible) If they were able to conduct reasoned analysis and grasp its fruits, the evidence would be in books. And there are no such books.*

> M: It is only through habit and an imposed social role that women are relegated to this lowly position. If they read, debated and asserted themselves more, men would have to allow them in.
> H: Oh, really?
> M: Women are mostly to blame for their own inferior status, often playing the very role men have decided for them: shallow, picturesque, always on the frivolous sideline of any serious discussion.

She, and other women, could always aspire: *I had rather die in the adventure of noble achievements, then live in obscure and sluggish security.*

While Margaret was writing to express frustrations at gender inequality, events across the Channel were forcing her pen in another direction — letters of condolence. She received news that her niece, then her eldest sister, Mary, had died of consumption. To compound her grief, Elizabeth Lucas died not long afterwards.

Margaret felt the tragedy of total separation from her mother who had done her best to provide for her children after the destruction of the family home. Margaret was in a *shipwreck wherein all happiness is drowned.* Death severed all connections. But it was not finished: news came that her half brother, Sir Thomas Lucas, had died from an injury.

Margaret was powerless to join her surviving brothers and sisters in mourning. Writing became her only way to deal with suffering, but her affirming '*Books are my offspring*' sounded like a plea in the face of a grim reality: she had not been able to conceive, a condition that may have stemmed from lack of exercise, or fasting and the regular purging of food.

Behind all this was the ever-present threat that William's

creditors would declare he had reached his limit. She could easily imagine women whose husbands played their entire estate away with dice and cards.

In straitened circumstances, Margaret could always slip through the narrow polar passage that led back to *The Blazing World*. And there it was again — a magic kingdom transcending the brutal, imperfect world from which she had come. Bringing herself, the Marchioness (later Duchess) of Newcastle, into the drama, she could act as a counterpart to the Empress — in the broader sense an advisor to all women that they are always free and able to create an imaginary reality, then alter it as they please. Her fish men could tow submarines and were indispensable, but her lice-men had endeavoured to weigh the air, which was absurd, so she dissolved their society: *Every human creature can create an immaterial world fully inhabited by immaterial creatures — all within the compass of the head or skull.*

The Blazing World was, of course, conceived largely in response to the imperfect world in which she lived:

> *All the world might be as one united family, without divisions. Otherwise it may prove as miserable a world as that from which I came, wherein are more sovereigns than worlds, and more pretended governors than governments, more religions than gods, and more opinions of those religions than truths, more laws than rights, and more bribes than justices, more policies than necessities, and more fears than dangers, more covetousness than riches, more ambitions than merits, more services than rewards, more languages than wit, more controversy than knowledge, more reports than noble actions, and more gifts by partiality, than according to merit; all which, said she, is a great misery.*

To prove William was ignoring the steepening slope of insolvency, a dinner was arranged with Descartes, Gassendi and Hobbes, Mersenne being too ill to attend.

Margaret chose a dress of green satin with metallic lace trim and a line of jet buttons, the boned bodice cut so low it looked in constant risk of slipping from her shoulders. Augmenting the roseate flush of her cheeks was a sash red enough to stain the men's retinas. A pendant that survived being pawned, gleamed from her cleavage. It was to be an ensemble none had seen before. Margaret designed her own attire, taking pleasure in the looking-glass of viewing herself while still fresh and young. When it came to innovation:

> *If not according as the fashion runs,*
> *Lord how it sets a-work their eyes and tongues!*

This time her mirror was telling her how folds of green sheen gave the illusion of a dress dipped in oil. The whole was tipping close to vulgarity, and she knew it. To kindle her husband's desire a wife should not *just act the courtesan*, she should rouse other men's envy. But this didn't preclude subtlety. Her fringe was an arc of spirals across her forehead that would remind a discerning scientific eye of shell helices, whirlpools of draining water, tiny ram's horns, or, in Descartes' case, the self-similar logarithmic curve he had plotted, now decorating his hostess.

To be looked at and only addressed with platitudes — this was her function at the all-male table. She sat next to William. Across from her Gassendi was the most challenged of the diners: having to follow the discussion and avoid William's eye while his own was drawn to the magnet of Margaret, charmed by the occasional glimpse of a rouged half moon of nipple.

Dinner was venison dressed in onion rings with bread and potatoes, a meal their resourceful chef saved from mediocrity with creamy syllabubs and a spiced apple blancmange. Most drank wine. Margaret risked a glass of Parisian water her staff insisted was boiled.

She remembered Descartes and Sir Charles starting a conversation on analytical geometry. She had tuned out, then some impulse of her duties as hostess stirred her from a trance where her glass in double vision regained its sharpness. Descartes was gesturing to Hobbes as he spoke.

'So how do you account for the nature of subjective, or first person, experience?'

'The world has length, breadth and depth,' said Hobbes. 'Spirits also have dimension, because they're bodies.'

'That's an evasion. We have subjective thoughts because we have a mind, which has nothing to do with the body.'

There was a pause, and Margaret had her filler ready:

The answer lies between the two. We are obviously material, or matter, but we can't understand how matter thinks.

Why didn't she just make the statement? Because she was unfortified by wine? William would be the last to object, so it must have been Mistress Bashful who had swallowed the words. Hobbes replied:

'You refer to an incorporeal substance, which is a contradiction in terms, a body without a body.'

'You misconstrue,' said Descartes. 'I'm saying that not all substances are bodies.'

But where does your immaterial spirit reside, Monsieur Descartes?

Descartes had large brown eyes that remained almost half closed, conveying part tenderness, part tiredness, and were thus inscrutable. She knew the mind behind them held a formidable intelligence, so it must have been the aquiline nobility of his nose that disclosed it, and the wide authority of a mouth that smiled in an understated way in response to insights, sharp rejoinders, feminine looks or sudden witticisms. His shoulder-length hair was cut short at the fringe to enclose his face in a circle of umber-coloured curls.

Sir Charles and William were discussing craters on the moon. Descartes and Hobbes saw an opportunity to abandon their quarrel.

'What has caused the craters?' asked Gassendi, who had his own answer but was keen to gauge reactions, hoping one would emerge from the succulent morsels of Margaret's lips.

'Volcanic activity?' said William.

'Impacts of meteors?' offered Sir Charles.

The flaws and stains of its stony body? she was about to say.

'Meteors, I think you're right,' Gassendi affirmed, benevolent, but with a touch of condescension. 'And what do you say to this: stars are suns with their own planets.'

Descartes was quick to seize the initiative:

'I think the Marchioness should answer.'

Margaret coloured, then said:

'If you can't settle the question yourselves, being so educated, then I cannot help. Anyway, women are as complex, as baffling to you, as the cosmos.'

No-one could see as William squeezed her knee.

Word came from Queen Henrietta that the Cavendishes were to re-locate to Holland. William had once been a guide and advisor to Prince Charles, and she hoped he could be of help in the eventual restoration of their crown.

Shifting the whole household came at great expense, necessitating further borrowing. Two passenger coaches were needed, carts for the family belongings, and several horses for servants. They left on a grey day scumbled with light cloud.

Sharing the smaller coach with William, Margaret had their ink-well fixed to the front wall to forestall spillage but permit dipping of the nib for notes en route. In her mind she ran through subjects from dinner table discussions with their eminent visitors, fascinated by the microcosmos of atoms and their scintillas of consciousness, that stars might be splinters of the sun long since ejected from their parent, and a lodestone the universal symbol of all attractive force.

Early in the journey she saw how light refracted through a crack in the carriage window projected a tiny rainbow onto the sill. Did this mean all colours hide in white light? Ideas were jotted down in an impassioned scrawl pocked with misspellings.

As their carriage passed through Compeigne, Margaret was re-reading William's poems.

> No man can love more or loves higher,
> Old wood and dry wood makes the best fire,
> Burns clearest and is still the same
> Turned all into a living flame.

She took his hand that had written those words, feeling its warmth. How lucky she was to marry this man, in spite of detractors like the imperious, ever-slappable Lord Widdrington, a royalist who had joined William in exile and cast a disapproving eye on Margaret: she was too young, inexperienced or low-born for him. But how could he know about the depth of their love, of her importance in William's life? *My mirth was his music, my smiles were his heaven, my frowns were his hell.*

Marriage allowed her to express the capabilities of her sex. She could make women wield power in imagined worlds, participating fully in scientific discovery and artistic endeavour. She could write roles for men, having them speaking her own words. Instead of reinforcing women's softness and passivity, she could make them proactive, even dominant, arousing desire in any man she encountered. Part of this was the allure of the foreign — the same feeling she had projected for painters of her portrait: exotic, enigmatic. If in the eyes of men there was a mystique about her sex, she would do her best to enhance it.

Their carriage passed through the breached fortifications of recently-besieged Saint Quentin, then onto fertile fields of the Cambresis. Some sights during the journey had the familiarity of any town or farm in England, but there were also different people, animals and buildings, suggestive in her writer's imagination of *The Blazing World's* sagacious menagerie:

The bear-men were to be her experimental philosophers, the fly-men, worm-men and fish-men her natural philosophers, the ape-men her chemists, the satyrs her Gaelic physicians, the fox-men her politicians, the spider-men and lice-men her mathematicians, the jackdaw-men, magpie-men and parrot-men her orators and logicians, the giants her architects, etc.

At Cambrai they were greeted by a jubilant crowd, their torches flaring in the dusky light. They could leave their coach while the horses rested. Margaret's choice for rest was the cathedral, where they were welcomed in by a carillon of bells, then their travel weariness was assuaged by the liquid tones of the church choir.

The next day they crossed the Deûle at Lille, then travelled on to Ghent, passing buildings of brown and red brick with stepped facades. Their journey ended at Antwerp, where William had found their new family home: a palazetto built by the painter Rubens. After four decades its grandeur had slightly crumbled. Loosened shingles made the house moan in the wind, and its rooms retained hints of camphor from an unlocatable source. Margaret could almost hear echoes of its past residents — voices preserved in leather wall-coverings, wood panelling and stairwells reiterated in a receptive part of her mind.

The property featured a gracious internal courtyard overlooked by three floors, and a baroque garden. Classical scholarship was referenced by a brotherhood of sculptures and trompe l'oeil of ancient Rome. With its baroque and Renaissance features, Rubenshuis stood waiting to receive what it deserved but the Newcastles lacked through financial embarrassment: lamps, tapestries and rugs, armchairs and cabinets, porcelain, paintings and tabletops of inlaid marble.

'What do you think of our new home?' asked William.

'It's fantastic. But . . .'

'What is it, my dearest?'

'I received a letter this morning. From England.'

She looked out onto the garden where tops of wispy conifers were waving in a gentle breeze.

'More bad news?'

'The masonry of my mother's vault has been desecrated.'

'Who would do such a thing? What could they possibly achieve?'

'There's more, William. It's my brother, Charles. You remember he was leading royalist troops in Essex.'

'Was he captured?'

'Yes. Then executed.'

⁓

Through no fault of its own, Rubenshuis was associated in Margaret's mind not just with the demise of her family in England but with the fate of King Charles. She had been laying out curtains in the drawing room with her maid. The brocade was damaged but ready to be re-stitched for hanging in the reception room. A letter was delivered conveying the news that following his imprisonment and trial, King Charles had been executed.

Margaret watched the maid cutting a fabric of burgundy red, the twin scissor-blades glinting in the sun. Outside, birds kept singing, oblivious of her horror. Rubenshuis — beautiful and accommodating, but indifferent.

She felt far removed, sequestered from her English home, from the need and duty to mourn with others over the King's death. Exile could last a lifetime. The monarchy might never be reinstated, the structures of class, entitlement, nationhood and sovereignty crumbling into disarray and anarchy. One by one she was starting to lose her family, but lacked authority to do anything about it. She could have been living in the Orient, in a different world. She still had William, a Marquess trapped in France without a farthing to his name.

William's estates in England were his only assets, his only surety against which he'd been borrowing. A decision was made for Margaret to join Sir Charles Cavendish in crossing the channel to either prevent the dissolving of his estates, or to recover a portion of his original wealth. She couldn't bear the thought of separation from her husband, but it was feasible she might even be entitled to a benefit, being the 'innocent' wife of a royalist traitor — anything to relieve their indigence.

More distressing than seasickness, sudden storms, or marauders off the coast seeking easy prey, were the stringent measures in place in ports to check everyone's identity. They used the last of their money in bribes, then travelled as unobtrusively as possible. Sir Charles found a copy of Cromwell's charge against the King and read it to her:

'The king has been found guilty of attempting (now in his most authoritative voice, and complete with gestures) to uphold in himself an unlimited and tyrannical power to rule according to his will and to overthrow the rights and liberties of the people.'

'From what we've learned en route, this describes the autocrat Cromwell himself.'

'Don't speak so loudly.'

'We can't criticise what has been imposed on us?'

'Of course. But there's a more present danger. I've heard spies and informers are well remunerated.'

Heeding these warnings, Margaret took refuge in a room in central London high above the street. It was a kind of sanctuary, but public protests outside, scuffles and troop movements, showed England was still on a war footing.

She wrote poetry. Sir Charles knew philosophy and poetry were Margaret's savoir faire, and supported her literary ambitions as much as her husband did. Both men appreciated what was intuitive, spirited and visionary in her writing. Sir Charles was constantly encouraging:

'It happens that the most inventive and perceptive minds lack value by conventional judgement because they're not conventional minds.'

What Margaret had gathered for publication was *Poems and Fancies* and *Philosophical Fancies*, which she dedicated to *all noble and worthy ladies*.

'Does this sound like cheap flattery to my intended audience?'

'No,' replied Sir Charles, 'just an honest indication of your readership.'

'I'm prepared for mockery, from both sexes. A book, in one way just a common, physical object, may act as a trespasser. It may intrude upon mens' sole right to publish.'

'And so deny you the right to free expression.'

'Men direct and control through the book. I feel like an inferiority who has fashioned a weapon that equals in effectiveness that of her masters.'

'If it is a cannon across their bows, I say well-done.'

Both Empress and Duchess of *The Blazing World*, being of one mind, would agree with him:

I had rather die in the adventure of noble achievements, than live in obscure and sluggish security — by the one I have glorious fame, by the other I am buried in oblivion.

Margaret's motive was clear: *I write it for my own sake, not theirs*. If this is true, then she thinks it fair to ask why she is publishing. Isn't it enough just to express herself with pen and paper and leave it there? No, other factors needed to be considered. She didn't want her mind to close like a fontanelle with no further ideas permitted. Also, after being excluded from the high table of men's intellectual discussion, putting words in print could be a kind of retaliation.

It is the only expression appropriate to her solitude — her beloved husband back in France, and London still reeling from civil strife. Writing was her way to deal with loss, loneliness, mistrust and adversity.

Then one day was an event like no other. She noticed the light starting to fade, which shouldn't happen in broad daylight. Looking from her window, she saw Covent Garden turn greenish and submarine. Inside, and out in the street, everything had cooled. Opening the curtains wide, she looked into the sky and there was the sun with a large black bite taken out of it. The feeling was portentous, uncanny, but in her poetic frame of mind she could read the big event as a cosmic proclamation: the heavens in sympathy with England's suffering.

Her brother-in-law picked up a publication, *Annus Tenebrosus: The Dark Year*, written by the astrologer William Lilly and published not long after the eclipse. With many fearful citizens thinking The Day of Judgement was at hand, Lilly hoped his informative almanac would be a best seller, the eclipse heralding earthquakes, pestilence, strange massacres and desperate tumults. For Margaret this forecast felt like the violent reaction of nature to Macbeth's murder of King Duncan — without a rightful monarch at the head, the fabric of reality would start to unravel:

Nature's actions are not only curious, but very various; and not only various, but very obscure.

There was another side. She had come across Lilly's kind before, fearmongers who seized on cases of injustice, strife or natural calamity and augmented them with so-called hidden evidence, producing dire predictions. Lilly knew of the public's propensity for fear and hysteria. He enjoyed being a false oracle, while those with a hunger for secret knowledge who followed him had their self-esteem boosted by association.

Prophets' presaging on the eclipse died down. Months passed and Margaret's verse became both goaded and disturbed by William's absence. She wondered if he had been faithful to her. Had he set up a *seraglio of young wenches*? Was he luring them with syrupy verse? In their situation, was it right for men to take other lovers?

She consoled herself that, with Sir Charles's help, this period in England would bear fruit: any way to free up even a fraction of her husband's estates would be a wifely duty fulfilled. But financial processes were painfully slow, and she feared William might be even more frustrated than her. Trapped, as she was, in London, *I shall not wonder that my beauty is thought dead, my embraces cold, my discourse dull, my company troublesome to him.*

She felt no less entitled than others of her age to feel the weight of melancholy. The malaise was ambivalent. On one hand, the intensity and longing conducive to her poetry writing, and the disappointment or unfulfilled desire conducive to philosophy. On the other, she felt trapped in the most confining of the four humours. Uselessness, stupidity, poverty, madness — all were associated with her sex. But wasn't melancholy also integral to the human condition? Wasn't she sharing with others a kind of corporeal punishment for something long forgotten, as in another life? So many people around her were suffering from the civil war: exhausted, wounded, dispossessed, bereaved.

Her work ready for publication, Margaret was suspended at the point of no return: to publish, or not? The part of her that had worked in private all these months in London felt both creative and fearless — in stark contrast to her socially taciturn side. She wanted her work out on view and as open to criticism as any male writer. *Fame is a great noise*, and she wanted it ringing in her ears. What impelled her was an extravagance, a lack of restraint — *I'll do it anyway.*

This immoderation also went into the book's production, sparing no expense. She could, or should, have used a male pseudonym, but was resolute — she would boldly enter the literary world of men as Margaret Cavendish, even if the outcome was infamy.

When she published *Poems and Fancies* and *Philosophical Fancies*, the reaction (especially from women) was vicious. Of course, many believed she had entered an arena reserved for men, and so thought her contrived and peculiar. Margaret was indeed *flung on the dunghill of scorn*.

Meanwhile, Sir Charles Cavendish was able to transfer some money from estates he had managed to retain, easing William's financial predicament.

'I think you've saved us,' said Margaret.

'It's the least I could do.'

'I'd imagined returning to Antwerp and finding my husband gnawing rat's bones in a garret.'

～

On her return to Antwerp Margaret celebrated the reunion with her husband, and the slight improvement in their financial position, by commissioning a new dress to her own design. It was a gown in mauve velvet with purls and spangles of silver. The modified Basqued bodice had a higher waistline than usual, and an open neckline that made the bust swell daringly upwards. Being far more costume than clothing, this made Margaret a composer of luxurious originality — some would say a fearless couturier, others that she was scandalous.

Suitably, the gown had its outing at Antwerp's theatrical Ash Wednesday event. Arriving by coach, as was her custom, she found herself amidst dancers, cross-dressers, musicians, acrobats and poseurs. She saw a snake-handler, fire-swallower and strongman, a caged leopard, a sorceress in whose head-dress was a caged bird, two monkeys on a chain, an ogre who frightened the children, and a chocolatier who gladdened them.

Church bells pealed, and townsfolk could be seen at every window of the tall facades overlooking the Grote Markt. On the other side of the square, the City Hall remained blank and stand-offish, as if disapproving of such frivolity.

It was a revelry of otherness, the diversity of humanity allowed free expression. In her eye-catching gown she could be, for a brief time, the warrior-heroine of *The Blazing World*. She called it a world of *fancy, or (as I may call it) fantastical, which if it add any satisfaction to you, I shall account myself a happy creatoress; if not, I must be content to live a melancholy life in my own world.*

Margaret had no shortage of strange and interesting real-life characters on which to draw, from the prying, opinionated Pepys to someone who left an impression on her life like no other — the recently-abdicated Queen Christina of Sweden. Hosting her at Rubenshuis, the young Christina looked out of place not just amidst the ornate wood and tiles, embellished windows, domed ceilings and Flemish leatherwork, but in her own clothing.

While Margaret followed the dictum that one's dress should never be prim and proper, but always have a well-considered smidgeon of the tawdry, the Queen's attire lacked both, being unkempt and decidedly unroyal. Surely the Swedish treasury had the funds to present her with more richness and style than this plain, tired-looking garment of glaucous green? Where were the jewel-encrusted brooch, the monogrammed ring, rouge make-up and coiffed hair?

One answer came with Christina's request to visit William's stables. Sharing his love of horsemanship, and keen on hunting, Margaret observed her guest in rustic dress springing to the saddle and testing a Cavendish thoroughbred at full gallop.

She liked Christina's directness, her conversation free of flowery phrases. But it was punctuated by coughs.

'Would you have a muckender, Margaret?'

'Sorry, a — ?'

'I need to blow my nose.'

Like a magician, William produced a lace-frilled handkerchief from nowhere, passing it to her with an elegant gesture.

'Thank you. A nose the size of mine carries copious sludge.'

Blowing it brought forth a long honk like a frightened duck.

'Excuse the music,' came Christina's insincere apology. 'Just a quinsy of the throat. No fikes, blains or scabs for you to catch, I assure you.'

'Shall we walk in the garden?' said Margaret.

1660. With a new decade, and the revitalising effect of spring, the Newcastles could take heart at a proclamation from across the channel: Charles II was now restored to the throne as the lawful monarch. The new Charles, observed William, was the necessary link between the state and the divine realm, ending a riotous and bloody vacuum that had lasted eighteen years.

Finally, the Cavendishes were able to sail home.

Though the boat that brought them to the continent didn't founder, it didn't make the return trip feel safer. A wind rushed up the channel from the Baie de la Seine, whipping the wave peaks, making the sea barrier between the two lands seem forbidding, and any seafarer reckless to attempt a crossing. She couldn't see England, lost in a grey haze. William must have felt her misgivings. With a chivalry natural to him, he helped her aboard and offered reassurances:

'Just a short hop, my love. This will put fresh air in your lungs. There are master seamen running this ship.'

They stayed out on deck, eyes on the horizon for the first sight of land, the emerging cliffs a solid, stable line above the rough and rolling sea.

Margaret felt her predestined life returning. Royalist exiles like themselves were rewarded not just with pensions or annuities, but regained most of their former estates.

She duly organised the repair and maintenance, from drapes and mullioned windows to the wide compass of gardens, the ironwork and crenellated towers. She calculated her husband's losses during the Civil War at nearly a million pounds, but there was no point in mourning this damage.

Their societal status was not just re-established, but improved: Charles II elevated the Cavendishes to the Duke and Duchess of Newcastle, a title that for Margaret was a vision from *The Blazing World* come true. William was also appointed Gentleman of the Bedchamber. Though she knew this was an honorific, Margaret was tempted to believe it was the unchaste public recognition of a spirited master and his passionate mistress.

A whole cycle of violence and disruption had ended. Hobbes provided philosophical support for the restoration, his *Leviathan* stating that civil law required a strong and stable monarchy, the sovereign the keystone preventing the structure from crumbling.

'And how is our old friend?'

'Hobbes? Plodding on, though his ailing frame has sustained a few shocks.'

'What shocks?'

'*Leviathan* could be in the firing line,' said William. 'A bill has passed the commons, against blasphemy and ungodliness.'

'Now you worry me my own work might be deemed ungodly.'

'No fear, my love. Unlike yours, Hobbes's writing delves into scripture. Knowing him, it will be —'

'Critical?' said Margaret.

'Certainly disparaging,'

'And clerics bristle at impiety. So he fears a heresy charge?'

'Exactly.'

'What can he do?'

'He deemed it prudent to set fire to any blameworthy papers.'

'Before they set fire to him?'

Margaret's official appearance after the restoration was genuine theatre. Her arrival in London had been covered by newsletters, the streets around Whitehall crowded with onlookers. Of the distinguished couple, Duchess Margaret commanded the most attention. She made no secret of seeking fame. Some flocked just to see her latest extravagant dress. Pepys's comment that she was crazy and conceited only increased her allure. She would never be jeered to death. Why not allow the gossipmongers free rein? It could only boost book sales.

For many in her position, such ostentation would be an embarrassment, but not according to Margaret Cavendish. Though being close to destitution in France, with the Restoration she had come into her own and was a blazing star of her own creation.

As if to make up for their previous penury, she travelled like a queen, in a cavalcade of three coaches, her own drawn by six of William's finest steel-shod stallions, this centrepiece 'guarded' in front by the men and behind by her ladies-in-waiting. The whole entourage, including the coachmen, were uniformed in a dignified yet ceremonious black and white, trimmed with strips of silver, while the dazzling Duchess had the feral embellishment of a long furred train that made her visit to court resemble a marriage more than a presentation to Charles II.

It seemed she was living in one of her fairy tales — her Empress in *The Blazing World* coming to life, luxuriating amongst wealth, adornment and abundance, after having ascended unhindered to a position of unchallenged sovereignty. The book had become a memoir in reverse, her writing about the much-fêted Empress, then having a title conferred upon her.

Meeting the King in the real world, she played this aristocratic game in her own way, mute, but dressed in fabulous style. While the entirely visual display matched the assertive, imaginative, often outrageous voice in her writing, she had no fear of bumbling verbal performance. That voice was locked in print, soundless.

An invitation for Margaret to attend the Royal Society of London was an honour, if a dubious one.

On one hand, the call for her presence was proper. Her brother, John Lucas, was a founding member of the society, and after her own recent publications *Philosophical Letters*, *Observations on Experimental Philosophy* and *The Blazing World*, wasn't this the right way to honour her? The first two books were pitched straight into the masculine academic sphere, while *The Blazing World's* imaginative conjectures veiled her serious commentary on science and patriarchal control.

For this reason she had some qualms about her reception at such an illustrious institution. If any of these gentlemen had read *The Blazing World*, they would have found a story veined with Margaret's fascination for the natural world and interpretations re-modelled to her parallel realm. They couldn't fail to feel the book's satirical sting. In her imaginary empire women were emancipated; here they were not. At its centre was the Empress — educated, principled, capable — and Margaret had sent her back to our defective world to vanquish brutal warmongers by using her far superior powers.

But the real Margaret still had a natural reserve, a coyness long embedded, ready to foil her ability to face off against these scientists and philosophers. Hobbes had been no help in ridding her of this reticence. At Mersenne's salon she feared he might find one errant thread in her argument and pull it, the gown of logic coming adrift, leaving her naked.

The one abiding injustice of her life was not being able to share ideas with men. Now it seemed they were ready to receive her.

She had an advantage no man had, refined by wealth, practice, an aesthetic eye, creativity and attention to detail: her dress and appearance should work as a calculated statement, a camouflage against attack. Was it better to downplay femininity so that sexual difference was less of a factor, or enhance it in defiance of her advancing age and natural shyness?

Clothes were forms of thought, after all: contemplations on herself, something aspired to, an artwork encasing the body. Could the ensemble work in collaboration with the attitude she had chosen to project? Given these ideas, she dismissed the neutral, charcoal-shaded linen in plain cut. It made her appear humble, nun-like and low-status. She favoured the other extreme, a picture of the

Empress in her story coming to mind. She settled on a salmon-coloured silk gown with lightweight boned struts and violet piping, the waist pulled into pleats like fluted, radiating petals of a daisy. While displaying the rise of her creamy bosoms, her bodice and its fence of violet lace managed, only just, to guard her nipples from public view. Here again was the couturier's statement: a costume hinting at hidden intensities beneath. Margaret's hair was curled to perfection, and her maid had spent an hour painstakingly severing her mistress's split ends with sharp scissors.

She selected a plain string of pearls, then a furred mantua for the journey. Hot resin smoked through her coiffure would outdo in subtlety any man's powdered periwig.

The weather was unruly and Margaret was late. Approaching the ground floor colonnade of Gresham College in her carriage, Margaret reviewed what her brother had said to expect from the Royal Society, apart from its relative newness and Charles II's patronage. Francis Bacon was the academic figurehead, the inspiration for scientific method and naturalist philosophy that were its guiding principles. Innovation was a keynote, testing of the natural world using the senses being the surest way to knowledge, rather than reading and absorbing other ideas, especially the ancients.

The Duchess Margaret Cavendish was received as an esteemed guest. The crowd of members, whether supportive of her presence or not, were all eager to see this famous lady — piquant and half preposterous — up close. Even the maids who trailed behind her were pleasing to the eye, although Margaret would have done well to leave the svelte, olive-skinned beauty, La Ferrabosco, behind, since she was drawing too much attention.

In the air was some chemical smell she couldn't identify, along with a friendly pomposity. First in the proceedings was the kind of ritual befitting a secret society: words and actions that sounded scripted, and a brief period of solemnity while those of apparently higher rank stood apart.

Then Robert Hooke, curator of experiments, led her through several exhibits as though she were Charles II's own consort or emissary, his voice echoing in the lofty space. Experimental showpieces set up for the Duchess's visit included investigations of colour, and observing meat dissolve in sulphuric acid.

Margaret's brother had told her to expect various apparatuses. This was indeed what she found: telescopes, timepieces, orreries, lenses and stands to test optical theories, and a collection of guns presenting the mechanics of firepower. Something struck her about the machines. They were so elegantly made, so functional and certain. Yet something was missing. They might illustrate the mechanism of human beings and other creatures of the natural world, but they were inanimate, leaden, repetitive. Through spring or winding handle they gave the semblance of possessing a vital force, but this was the very thing they lacked. Further, since men were the machine-makers, didn't this impugn them with the same mechanical quality of predictable rationality?

Margaret hoped her flicker of disdain was missed by any who were studying her. She knew she certainly couldn't vocalise such a judgement without creating a scandal and being ushered off the premises. Shelving her thoughts for later contemplation, she returned to sustaining a demeanour of wonder, of curiosity, as she regarded the apparatuses several scientists were keen to elucidate.

Equipment, instruments, devices — she could understand the world view for which these were the showpieces. She saw the pragmatism, passion and skill that created them in this age of increasing scientific discovery. While stopped at an instrument fashioned in brass, with lenses and a winding mechanism for adjusting focal length, she said, mostly to herself:

'Hmm. An idea given outward form.'

'Madam?' said Hooke.

'Just a thought about the concept and . . . reality.'

The room went quiet. The Duchess had initially attracted attention for her sculpted hair, salmon-coloured gown and stately bearing. That attention doubled now she had actually commented on an exhibit.

'Could you explain yourself?' asked one of the men nearby, his grey breeches, polished boots and leather coat giving him the rural look of a country squire.

'I mean that it shows, objectively, the purpose and power of the mind that invented it,' she replied, hearing the quaver in her own voice now the conversation was public.

'You don't mean placeless mind where an immaterial soul should dwell?'

'No, sir. I mean mind that is everywhere part of nature and has its own means of organisation, one of its many marvels being . . . this construction we're now observing.'

Did he judge her approval of one of the contrivances as a means of ingratiating herself into this illustrious company? He continued:

'A most commendable attempt by the fair sex to account for the universe in some wise contrary to informed opinion.' His forced grin cast about for support.

'Which is?' she asked.

'That it is exclusively material, and mentality or spirit an airy nothing.'

'I advanced precisely this view in my *Philosophical and Physical*

Opinions, just four years past, but have become loath to defend the dead and stupefied world of mere materiality.'

Hooke couldn't suppress a laugh, and it was not in derision of her assertion. The 'squire' had taken a body blow, but went on:

'Clearly it takes some courage lacking in fickle feminine wit to accept the foregone conclusion of well-reasoned argument.'

She hoped her powdered cheeks would cover her flush at the affront, but had a reply:

'It would be vain to deny women the capacity to read and reason, or be cowed by any uncomfortable conclusion. Natural phenomena can not be accounted for through blind mechanism. I would be interested to hear how you, good sir, could prove that all things in nature lack mental properties.'

There was a murmur of approval from behind her. At this juncture Hooke, her unofficial guide, found a convenient distraction in one of his images of an insect, transcribed from a microscope and pinned to a display board. It was very large, mechanical-looking and grotesque. Pointing, and with the lightest pressure on her elbow, he said:

'Now here's a different manner of being to study.'

The squire, piqued that the Empress should have the last word, retreated to feign close study of a firearm, and fume.

Could one unchallenged comment by Margaret, in public and surrounded by men of science, be considered a significant victory? For once she had thrown off the fetters of diffidence and doubt that so hampered her verbal exchanges.

Now, in the carriage and returning home, she thought of those men she had left behind, admiring their endeavours irrespective of gender disempowerment. All those precision instruments, theories, planetary models, books, charts and equations — what was the ultimate nature of the reality they were all so passionately seeking, herself included? If all was physical, in what were her molecules suffused? Since her heart was beating inside wider rhythms — circadian, menstrual, seasonal, annual — what was the final, all-inclusive tempo?

She still had the glow of fulfilment at being understood, or somehow accepted by the Royal Society. Yet at the heart of it all she didn't understand herself. How could a whole life depend on a world that was, at root, incomprehensible?

Through the carriage window she could see a star, fixed in the void behind parting clouds, blazing into its strange worlds, like the one she had created with words. At the same time, her hands lightly clasped, her thumb could sense the tiny pulse in her wrist, going on, faithfully, to the end: 1 . . . 2 . . . 3 . . . 4 . . . 5 . . . 6 . . . 7 . . .

Undoubtedly

IT WAS A MEADOW in the Netherlands, yet nowhere he would recognise as the Netherlands. They were walking where the meadow sloped down to a river and a kind of open kitchen, a table with basketware and a pitcher, and out on the river, drifting in the current, fishermen casting their nets.

Francine was talking to someone he couldn't identify, but their conversation faded as he turned to take in the meadow: a living presence, long grasses swaying and growing, the river carrying duration in its current. He could step down next to it and watch minutes passing by over stones. This kitchen was homely, promising. Shouldn't it be the nucleus of a rural idyll, a place for communion and sustenance? He turned to Francine, seated on a barrel, a red rash prickling her face, her fists beating the sides of the barrel like a drum.

A staccato of pummelling dragged him from the fleeting encounter. He came to in the cold air of a darkened room, feeling the image of his magically-revived daughter sinking back into the past, but the love remaining, stronger than ever. Her brief presence brought a lump to his throat, while his reasoning mind confirmed, through the dream's compelling theatre, the timeless, placeless condition of the incorporeal self.

Again a series of thumps on the door, followed by the night warden calling his name. He managed a response:

'Anon. Anon. I hear your confounded percussion, sir.'

The early riser was Rene Descartes. He had woken into a chamber in Tre Kronor, the Royal Palace in Stadsholmen, Sweden. The year was 1649.

He couldn't keep the Queen waiting, but this was such an imposition — being forced to rise at five, a full four hours before the city's birds celebrated the dawn. He had always slept until at least ten, a habit perfected since his childhood at La Flèche. It was his version of a constitutional, sure to be conducive to good health, as well as the formulating of new insights.

He had been curled like a cat round a small ball of warmth, but now as he dressed, he felt a chill flowing under the heavy oak door, numbing his feet, rising into his bones.

He lit the candle and moved next to the steel mirror, the metal sheen clear enough to see bloodshot eyes and grey streaks in his thinning hair. And what of the neatly-arrayed knowledge behind those tired eyes? There were numerical structures and environs of related scientific facts; there were long-nurtured ideas that had sprouted in the fertile earth of France and the Netherlands. Once his brain had thawed he would be back among them all.

Still, the urge to return to bed was strong. For heaven's sake — he was a full thirty years older than the Queen — didn't that give him some authority? But he was her guest, by invitation, and protocol demanded he fulfil the simple duty of a four-hour tutorial before Christina moved on to affairs of state. After that, he could sleep all he liked. But he wouldn't. Why waste the few precious hours of daylight?

He heard himself sigh with resignation, then finished dressing, drew his robe around him, and left the room, consoling himself that there were two small benefits in this arrangement: the warmth of a log fire, and a largely unplanned journey of philosophical discussion.

Christina hadn't the slightest interest in displaying the feminine charms of a twenty-three year old Queen. There she was, lit by the orange glow of the fireplace and a candelabra arranged by her ladies-in-waiting, shod in a man's boots, her hair an unruly mass of knots and curls.

Descartes had never seen the likes of her before: an aristocrat with none of the finery or displays of wealth, and none of the lofty rhetoric affecting the powerful. Instead, she could utter some of the crudest language he had ever heard.

But this was far from the full measure of the young lady. Her mind was sharp, and hungry for knowledge of languages, politics and metaphysics. She had expanded the palace library, a resource for which Descartes was most grateful, and helped establish Stadsholmen's first newspaper. She had invited scholars like himself to make the palace a forum for the very newest ideas. Like sunrays glistening on the snow outside, her wish was for a Tre Kronor scintillating with intelligence.

'I'm like an infant eager for the paps.'

'Excuse me, madame?'

'I wish to know more of the methodic doubt we touched on yesterday.'

'Simply the philosopher's quest for certainty.'

She gestured with her boot at a log crackling and sparking in the grate.

'You wouldn't question that this fire was real?'

'I'm grateful it warms the blood Your Highness, yet combustion lacks solidity. A most singular phenomenon of reduction.'

'Not likely the thoughts of heretics first feeling the flames.'

'Indeed, so I will evade the example.'

The Queen leaned in, more intently this time.

'I assume, then, you sought to find out all that can be doubted?'

'True.'

'What of that door closing just seconds ago. You heard it?'

'I did, but might it not have been a distant cannon?'

'And the candelabra at your elbow?'

'Solid enough, but invisible in the darkness and when out of range. A temporary artefact a furnace would reduce to an ingot.'

'I'll warrant what can't be doubted is the stench of some mewling shite-a-bed.'

'Indeed Your Highness, but some mothers may bear the mixed fortune of lacking this sense.'

'So all of this is subject to doubt?' she said, her hand describing a not inelegant arc around the chamber with its hung tapestries, heavy furniture and arched windows.

'Insofar as it changes or disappears when I am asleep, yes, even this is questionable.'

'And what of nipple-hardening sensuality, of beauty — surely it cannot be discredited. Think of the exquisite Countess Ebba, whom you have met. This quality can never be denied.'

Descartes had already cast doubt on the reliability of Platonic forms, but could hardly imply errors of judgement by the Queen, especially in affairs of the heart. He said:

'There's no mistaking the soul's delight in the beauties of nature, even its nourishment from them. And you're perceptive in approaching the crux of the issue.'

'You mean the guts of it, of what is certain in all circumstances?'

'Exactly. Reason, the faculty men like to say is in their province, arrives at the same conclusion as the feminine intuition.'

'That men are upstanding vertebrates and women fat-arse jellyfish with quaggling teats?'

He was taken aback at the comment.

'I'm sorry,' she said. 'Take no notice of me. But the crux of the issue is . . . ?'

'Thought. Just thought. Irrefutable, always manifest. Isn't this the surest indicator of our existence?'

'Very well, Monsieur Descartes. But while I know I'm thinking, this leaves me in some doubt I am the Queen of Sweden.'

He didn't like this slippery avenue, but she smiled, then said:

'And another certainty for you, now you're acquainted with me: I warrant you've never met such a muck-spout woman in all your travels.'

Self-deprecation always brought her royal majesty down to earth. There was never any status tension with the Queen of Tre Kronor's towers, no cause for genuflection, forced smiles or caution over an accidental blasphemy. It amused him how their conversation jumped so readily from splendid to sordid, but he respected her eagerness for knowledge. So young, she could have been Francine, had his dear girl lived. There was always this reminder, so, as convention demanded, he maintained a respect for the Queen — the same reverence as for a disembodied spirit called Francine.

～

Through an arched window in the Tre Kronor tower, Descartes could see the castle's finials piercing the cold grey sky, their flags limp and frozen. In the distance a church spire, a huddle of buildings, then two ships, bare-masted, in the iced-up grip of this corner of the Baltic. It felt like a place of exile. Or incarceration.

Were it not for his obligation to Her Majesty, at this time of late morning he would still have his head on the pillow, his body in a cocoon of warmth, his pen recording thoughts on the *Passions de l'ame*, nose attendant on the first whiff of his daily omelette rising from the kitchen.

Monsieur Chanut had a lot to answer for. The French ambassador, also his friend, was enamoured of the Queen. His letters had been full of praise. Writing from France, then Holland, Descartes established good terms with the Swedish court and could see an escape route from church persecution.

Now, in the Tre Kronor tower, he cringed at his own obsequious response to Christina's invitation. Like the flame flickering in an alcove behind him, the twisting flow of his letter to Chanut had made its own attempt to warm the castle's stone and the Queen's heart:

I hereby declare to Your Majesty that there is nothing so difficult that she might command me to do that I should not always be ready to accomplish it, and that if I had been born a Swede I could not be more devoted.

When Christina sent a warship commanded by Admiral Fleming to receive him, the philosopher could hardly refuse. With such authoritative transport laid on he had to dress appropriately, and chose his usual black garb with sharp-toed shoes and newly-curled hair. The naval flagship and her high-ranking commander helped allay earlier travel fears of drowning in a storm or being waylaid by bandits.

Perils of a different kind awaited.

'Now you have come to my court,' Christina had said, you must see more of Sweden. The journey north to Uppsala and west to the lakes of Orebro, perhaps.'

'But —'

'Six weeks should be enough.'

Is this your flavour of banter, he felt like saying: me, with metal-spiked boots, a frozen compass and scant furs, close to the North Pole, a lumbering white bear stalking me through the sleet?

'That's very kind of Your Majesty. I will think on it.'

The lie that he would accomplish whatever she instructed, along with Chanut's blandishments about the young Queen, had bitten back. Though keen to take barometric readings at this arctic latitude, there would be high enough pressure from the court to test his wits.

He sensed trouble from bigots at court, who saw Sweden as a strictly Protestant country and Descartes a scheming Catholic interloper. He read this message daily in the looks of suspicion cast in his direction. Many would know his books were banned by some authorities in the Catholic Church, labelling him a dissident, if not a heretic.

Now he was ensconced at Tre Kronor, Descartes considered his chances of being arraigned. Visitors like himself were immune from arrest and subsequent execution for beliefs at odds with strict Lutheran orthodoxy, yet that could change at any time. Was Christina a zealot? He thought not. But it was in her hands.

For this, and the threat of an arctic expedition, staying in bed was the wisest course of action.

But there was always the library. After breakfast, and when the weak sun had risen in cursory acknowledgement of dwellers in the frozen north, Descartes continued his exploration of the Queen's bookshelves. One bank was full of manuscripts, some sophisticated, others turgid. He found rolled papers on Swedish history kept in leather cylinders.

When it came to the books, the marginalia were more interesting than the printed text. He wondered whether Christina or her father Gustav Adolph was responsible for the volumes on epicurism and raising chickens, but had no illusions as to who had added vulgar jokes here and there in the same cursive script.

Unloading several heavy volumes in red leather from a wooden trunk was the royal librarian and one-time Professor of Eloquence at the University of Uppsala, Johann Freinsheim. His jowly face and upwardly-tweaked moustache conveyed a thespian look.

'New acquisitions?' asked Descartes.

'By the thousand.'

'To bolster Tre Kronor's assets?'

Freinsheim managed a sour grin, then looked about and lowered his voice:

'Bolster, yes, and radically deplete Emperor Rudolf's library.'

'Ah, they were seized in Prague?'

He nodded. 'War booty.'

'And it's your task to —'

'Catalogue them. Not enough hours in the day.'

'I'm sorry.'

Descartes could smell the leather, mixed with a briny note from their passage by sea. He had known Freinsheim for some time, by correspondence. Like Chanut, the librarian had given Descartes a positive recommendation to travel north, reassuring him there was no danger in being a Catholic cast among venomous Swedish Lutherans.

Descartes didn't share his optimism. He couldn't unwrite his books, just as he couldn't expunge his fame as a scientist and philosopher. For some hardliners it didn't matter if he were criticising beliefs of a different denomination, he was still a doubter and detractor. Sweden had seemed to offer an escape from these anxieties, but now he had stepped into another kind of prison.

He would be closely monitored.

Descartes picked up a book on Seneca, an area of his colleague's expertise.

'You're still a tutor to the Queen?'

'Like yourself.'

'I hear she has a sudden appetite for biblical languages.'

'It's a slow plod. Slower because of this literary mountain.'

'I can't help but feel some pleasure in this vast acquisition,' said Descartes, 'despite Prague's loss and your administrative burden.'

'Understood. But am I handling stolen property?'

'Not if plunder leads to intellectual cultivation of the victors. Might not this library change hands in the same way at some time hence, moving by conquest across Maghrib or the Levant, informing new and different intellects?'

'The sooner the better.'

Descartes resumed his tour of the shelves, hoping Christina would make all this public knowledge more accessible to enquiring minds than Emperor Rudolf had done. It puzzled him how these ink-encoded pages could convert to abstract 'knowledge' and reconfigure the faculty of reason. His own books would have this power, just as communicable and enabling now as in a hundred years' time.

He continued into a new alcove of books. Some were conducive to a kind of digressive meditation, his mind finding byways only tentatively implied by what was read, or not implied at all. What recurred was something for which the book was only a tenuous trigger — the same way the dream of his lost daughter, Francine, had flowered in a field, in his mind, by its own volition.

Eleven years had passed since she was taken by scarlet fever. He had started to forget her face, a face blurred with something artificially constructed, the real features elusive, melting away.

What of his role as father? Was he not attentive enough to her? Could his knowledge as a physician have saved her? Were it not for her death, he would have her with him now. Instead, it was this strange substitute: the sovereign Christina.

For two days a blizzard swept over the city. Sleet angled in, turning the town diagonal, gathering into clumps on spires, crenellations and windowsills. The wind it rode on made hollow, portentous moans down chimneys and passageways of the stone structures. Descartes pulled his coat tighter, arms rigidly folded in an attempt to generate heat.

After the smothering chill he was eager for some clarity, some overview. As he climbed to the south side of the central tower to watch the last rays of the setting sun, Descartes noticed Chancellor Axel Oxenstierna approaching. It was a distant corner of Tre Kronor, so he wondered if he had been followed. At sixty-six the Chancellor was thirteen years his senior and the steps had proved a challenge: the man was out of breath, his joints crackled, and he had a pronounced stoop. Notwithstanding these disabilities, he retained a mien of authority — Christina's only rival for state power. Black robes and a skullcap gave him an ecclesiastical air.

'Monsieur Descartes.'

'Good-day, sir.'

'The lessons with her highness, how are they faring?'

'Most satisfactory.'

The Chancellor coughed, halfway between an expostulation and genuine throat clearing, then asked:

'Does your tutelage in philosophy include any ... admissions by her Majesty ('Majesty' being delivered with a hint of contempt) of a personal nature?'

'I don't ... Could you be more specific, sir?'

'Her father, bless his departed soul, would be hoping for an heir.'

'Quite.'

'But not a hint of marriage in the offing. Storkyrkan Cathedral stands waiting for the nuptials, as does everybody in the land.'

'I'm sorry to hear that, sir.'

'The woman has no ambition.'

Descartes had little interest in becoming involved in power struggles at Tre Kronor. A few courtiers had given him looks as icy as a Stadsholmen morning, but he ignored them. The Queen was openly admiring of her friend Ebba Sparre, La Belle Comtesse, as she was known, and if this was where her affections lay, in Sapphic love, then he wished her well. With her fair skin, rosy cheeks and crowning glory of light brown hair, the Comtesse was a magnet for the eyes.

Oxenstierna's head was inclined to the side like a magistrate about to pronounce judgement, one eye fixing him from under a bristled brow.

'I have no qualms of confidence in your ability to tutor the Queen, Monsieur Descartes. But may I offer some advice?'

'Of course.'

'You'll do well never to point out that she is wrong. She'll give off sparks. Secondly, never compliment her on her looks, clothing or feminine charms. She holds no store by them. And third, you'll know this already, her tongue shapes the current of a sewer-ditch.'

'Her language is certainly... spirited.'

Descartes could read it more in the chancellor's eyes than in what he had said. This man, a veteran of military strategy, pragmatic and with the interests of Sweden paramount, was also a reluctant patriarch. His upstart twenty-three year old 'daughter' was asserting herself, probably jealous of his power and experience.

Descartes smiled to himself that the Chancellor was more than likely wearied by Christina, his bearing and aura showing the disintegration that comes with age, a man exhausted not only from his responsibilities, but tired of life. And Oxenstierna would have agreed with those who thought only men were capable of effective rule, especially those whose characters had been forged in war.

But didn't Christina sit on the throne? Wasn't she old enough to decide Sweden's future? Descartes had to think carefully how to phrase his next thought.

'There must have been a... somewhat patriarchal role in your relations with the Queen, if I may venture the opinion.'

'The role of surrogate father was waiting for me, but once out of childhood she would have none of it. Christina was only six when her father died, in battle. She'd just written to him, and I remember her words because her father read them to me: *I pray God will send us good news of Your Majesty, and I commend you to His protection.*'

'Gustav Adolph's reputation was undisputed: gentlemanly, refined, a great soldier,' said Descartes.

'So, the greater loss for her.'

'And what of her mother?'

'Maria Eleonora. Still alive. But mother and daughter are estranged.'

'May I venture to ask why?'

'She was . . . touched, if you follow. At one stage we deemed it prudent to have her put into custody, at Gripsholm Castle, on an island a few days ride from here.'

'I take it maternal interest was lacking?'

'Certainly irregular. Christina was known to escape insults by riding horses and retreating into books.'

'Then she was like an orphan.'

'I suppose so.'

The winter sun was sinking, casting a pale-yellow square onto the curved stone wall he stood beside. Descartes was tired. He thought of the early morning session with the Queen, then the possibility she might have other commitments allowing him to lie in until ten. The euphoria of postponement.

The next morning was even colder, the warden's five o'clock knock even louder. Breaking into the serene suspension of sleep was profoundly disorienting. His thoughts felt sluggish, frigid. Splashing his face from a stone basin of icy water was one way to shock the system into life.

'My apologies, Your Highness. I'm late.'

She turned to the clock, a fine example in black marble with gold detailing.

'Exactly seven minutes. It is a trifle.'

Descartes made a slight bow in response, pondering for a second that those ever-ticking hands, obedient to the precision of springs and gears, had introduced the concept of lateness. Her eyes still on the clock, she said:

'Those hands aren't too different from our own. I recall a line from Thomas Hobbes: life is but a motion of limbs.'

'Indeed, Your Highness. I've met the gentleman who said it. The proposition is that our bodies operate by mechanical principles. I've studied these mechanisms in flayed animals.'

'You've observed the brawnes?'

'Yes, how food digests —'

'The makings of a turdy-gut?'

'Quite. And the reflexes, how the bones articulate and tendons pull. The beasts are essentially animated viscera.'

'Then we are the same, are we not?' she said.

'With respect to our bodies, we are.'

'And what of those who more resemble the beasts, who suckle at their teats if you will: the clodpate, the ruttish codshead?'

She must have noticed the perplexity in his eyes, just as he noticed the pertness in hers.

'By degree they might well be closer to the beasts, but by God's grace we humans, having intellect, are different in kind.'

'We . . . reside in this mechanism?'

'It is our condition, Your Highness. A soul dwelling in a body. And we can not only reflect on the body machine, but construct our own machines as well. My colleague, Pascal, recently contrived a mechanism capable of calculation.'

He noticed the Queen engaged in thought, perhaps missing his last remark. She walked away from the fire some distance, then turned and said:

'It is established then. We have a soul and intellect the beasts lack, but we are alike in having a bodily mechanism.'

'True.'

'I find this hard to believe.'

Her huge eyes were catching the firelight. There it was, the assertiveness Oxenstierna had said to be wary of, dancing on each shiny cornea Be careful, he told himself: *she'll give off sparks.*

'Really, Your Highness? Perhaps you could —'

'Intuition tells me the beasts cannot be mere machines. We kill animals daily in order to live, but I have never killed even a rooting swine without feeling sympathy for it.'

'Well —'

'Sympathy, Monsieur Descartes, for a grunting, flop-eared pouch of pork.'

'Your attitude is admirable. But may I tell you of certain experiments I have conducted?'

'So long as you don't bedash the beasts with too much logic.'

'I will try not to. My point is that we cannot render mere matter sentient. Or, to put it the other way: how can the mind be reduced to mere matter?'

'And the strutting human can so account for every *other* living thing?'

'We account for human beings' uniqueness in two ways: we have language, and we have reason.'

Christina pulled at a knot in her hair, flashed him another look, then said:

'And that so neatly eliminates the organic?'

'Dissection has shown me mechanical control of the wings of a bird, the tail of a fish, the claws of a cat. Think of a church organ; its harmony depends on the air from the bellows, the pipes that make the sound, and distribution of air in the pipes. You see, the real thing reduces to a machine.'

'Your organ is but a stallion's pizzle.'

With this the Queen ended the lesson.

Crossing the Tre Kronor courtyard he had to take care not to slip on the ice, an act of instinct and coordination while his deeper self fumed at his peremptory dismissal. The plan had been to avoid Christina's resorting to rude rejoinders by a quick lesson in anatomy, the node of transfer between mind and body: a small gland, the pineal, deep in the brain...

Now here was this mysterious pea-sized pod of viscera mediating the philosopher's unsteady gait, testing his mechanics across the icy cobbles.

The altercation had an unexpected blessing, with Christina preferring not to engage his services, thus allowing him blissful lie-ins with several of Freinsheim's newly acquired volumes.

But the lull was brief, the Queen having been distracted by plans for her birthday function, a stately ballet to take place in a grand hall specially fitted out for the event. Not so threatening, it would seem — except that he had been requested to perform.

Was this a pay-back, some cruel joke, where he would have to prance like an uncoordinated popinjay, a figure of ridicule for an audience of French scholars and other dignitaries? He could imagine the barbed epithets uttered by the Queen to those gathered around her. Descriptions of Descartes the terpsichore, amplified by gossip-mongers, would fast become the chatter of salons right across Europe.

Neither Chanut, Freinsheim nor Oxenstierna could offer advice on how to extricate himself from the humiliating task ahead.

'When she gets an idea in her mind... All part of a harmless celebration... You have to admit her creative flair when dealing with adversaries...' None of these responses helped.

Descartes had to employ some creative imagination. Knowing

the Queen, surely he could come up with some strategy to save his reputation? First he would have to appease her. But then what? An offer to help the proceedings in some other way? He was certain any toadying would only confirm her scheme to embarrass him, thus confirming the wisdom of making Descartes dance.

He decided some self-deprecation might help.

'Much as I appreciate Your Majesty's invitation that I should join the performance, I have to admit my skill in tempo, balance, fouetté and rebound are close to non-existent. The thought of a ballet ruined by my shambling efforts, quite apart from how age has slowed me, is not to be risked if the occasion of your birthday is to be the success you expect and deserve.'

Her eyes, more polar blue in this light than he had yet seen, held him for a few moments. Did she read his excuse as genuine, obsequious, or perhaps ironic? At least she could save face by employing him in a less physical capacity.

'In fact, I've been reconsidering your role,' she lied. 'I would like you to write the libretto for the ballet.'

The relief! He could hear choirs in full voice.

'I'll be only too happy to write it,' he lied.

Learning that the theme was *The Birth of Peace*, it didn't take much insight to realise this display was for Oxenstierna, who had been directing war operations for as long as Christina could remember. Wars were all about male power; she wanted to challenge it with this artistic statement.

She prescribed gallantry mixed with levity, but in Descartes' hands it was to be quite different. Instead of a troop of dashing soldiers in jovial spirits, he aimed for some realism — a ragtag procession of the walking wounded. It was not the kind of writing he was accustomed to and ran to several abandoned drafts, but Ambassador Chanut had faith that his friend could deliver something worthy of the occasion.

'Most importantly,' he said, 'it is written by a literary genius, even if performed by a pack of dilettantes.'

On the day, the ballet hall was blazing with torches. The French scholars dressed in their finest. Their expectations for the dinner, passed on to Christina with the utmost diplomacy, then to the cooks, were born of their disappointment with standard Swedish fare. Sauerkraut and slabs of unsliced reindeer simply wouldn't do. Since the Queen's purpose was for Sweden to become the jewel of European culture and learning, the culinary arts had also to meet high standards.

Given time to find all the best ingredients, including spices from India and the Far East, the Queen's birthday guests were treated to capons, pheasant and beef cooked with cinnamon, cloves, pepper and nutmeg. Traditional dishes of smoked fish and tarts with lingonberry jam were presented on elegant stoneware, along with a selection of breads, and soups in mazers. Women sipped from cups of sweet sack or cider, while the men preferred beer from pewter mugs, or balloons of French brandy. Tabletops clothed in lace rested on braced trestles for the laden tureens, silver platters and porringers.

This grand hall behind Tre Kronor's walls was an island of warmth, light, finery and gourmandising; outside the walls was another world, ruled by cold and hunger.

After such a satisfying dinner, and its intoxicating drinks, the ballet as centrepiece was virtually assured of a warm reception. Descartes pitched the work between true-to-life brutality and ironic grandiloquence. He was his own worst critic, yet *The Birth of Peace* met with a positive response, sufficient for him to be asked to write another work.

Dreamt up by the Queen, it was to be a stage-play fantasy set in Scandinavia, centred on a princess, her lover, and a villain who threatens their happiness. It builds to the lovers evading capture by concealing themselves under rough country dress — surprisingly similar to the apparel favoured by Queen Christina.

If the work had been completed it would surely have been the most unusual of Descartes' oeuvre, but he was diverted into the more scholarly task of producing statutes for the Queen's Swedish Academy. This was valuable work, yet ultimately a waste of time — the Academy never came to fruition.

In the feeble midday sun, against the north wall of Tre Kronor's interior courtyard, Descartes noticed Chancellor Oxenstierna's dismissal of two uniformed soldiers, who had been standing at starched attention in front of their commander, before he started climbing the steps to the colonnade above.

The Birth of Peace was over, but Descartes hoped the Queen's attempt to weaken her Chancellor's power at the castle hadn't weakened his own relationship with the great man. He caught up with him, his opening remark ready. But the Chancellor sensed his approach and was quicker:

'Duties now discharged for this ballet, Monsieur Descartes?'

'By God's grace. I'm not a military man but —'

'War is about the battle-scarred, not those who serve their country?'

Looking down on the philosopher from his greater height, Oxenstierna adjusted his brown velvet hat and awaited the response. A pair of kitchen staff passed carrying a wicker cage full of anxiously yawping fowl.

'I underwent military training in my youth,' said Descartes, keen to set the record straight. 'I respect those like yourself long-schooled in the arts of war, but know too the destruction it can wreak.'

'This may be —'

'You'll appreciate as well that Her Majesty assigned me this ... challenging role.'

'It is only unfortunate that Sweden's gains went unrecognised: our control of western Pomerania, the indemnity settlements and much more. How else can we pay for extravagances such as the ballet?'

'Agreed. That should not go unnoticed.'

'It is regrettable that the Queen chooses not to discriminate between what is in the Crown's carefully-managed coffers and what is assigned to her, the latter being substantial enough.'

'Hmm,' replied Descartes in thoughtful-looking sympathy. 'Improvidence.'

'No, profligacy,' said the Chancellor, and began efforts to mount the steps to the colonnade.

There was no preventing it, thought Descartes, as he watched him ascend. Those with illustrious careers will start to creak, malfunction and die, handing on the world to younger strengths. It applied as much to himself as to Baron Axel Oxenstierna.

Winter deepened. Days grew even shorter, the sun paying only faint respect to Stockholm's citizens before plunging them back into darkness. Freinsheim had escaped his arduous cataloguing and travelled south. It was easy to imagine him on the coast of Spain where, so they said, never a snowflake has fallen.

Descartes thought he had taken the measure of the cold at Tre

Kronor, but the temperature kept dropping. He awoke, shivering in the pitch blackness. It brought back the intuition he'd had in Egmond before boarding Admiral Fleming's vessel, that it would be a mistake to go to Sweden. The interminable arctic journey past Öland, Västervik and berg-encased Norrköpings Bukten gave the air an ever more brittle quality, his nose, ears and fingers turning a numbed purple. Everything was frozen solid, including his mental processes and motivation. He felt his heart's hard slog trying to keep the distant capillaries of his machine at functioning temperature.

Sweden — a mistake? The Netherlands was his home, while Sweden was unknown. He hadn't bothered to research tenets of the Lutheran faith, but did file away comments from the court he was meant to overhear:

'Rumours circulate about an invasion from Rome.'

'Closer than that. From Poland.'

'Some say there are Catholic missionaries in our midst.'

'With orders direct from the Pope.'

'So why doesn't the Queen enforce the anti-Catholic rule?'

The idea of his being anti-Protestant wasn't just tedious, it was dangerous. Therefore Sweden was dangerous, and not only about religious belief but also the unforgiving winter. He had learned to trust intuitions, and wondered now: What lay behind that sudden flash of advice from nowhere which he hadn't heeded? Did intuitions ever come with reasons attached? Or was that just the point, that each was a distinct source of knowledge? What had the insight been: Don't trust Chanut's advice, or don't trust the Queen? No, the threat was much more immediate: the physician in him realised that if he got too cold he would become susceptible to a fatal respiratory illness.

Should he try to get out of the contract with Christina? Forgo what was still a generous remuneration? And then what? Return to France, or the Netherlands, where a case against him might be reopened by church authorities? At least Stockholm carried no such danger. Or not yet.

Lying awake, it didn't take too long for that triad of dreams from his youth to return. It was almost thirty years to the day. He had gone to bed to escape the winter cold in a German town, but that bedroom, unlike this one, had been blissfully warm thanks to an efficient stove.

He dreamt, vividly remembering three separate visions. The first had him caught in a cyclone where he managed to find shelter with an old friend. Strangely, the friend offered him a melon he had somehow obtained from a tropical country. Jolted back to wakefulness, he was convinced this particular scenario, and its strange fruit, had been implanted in his mind by an evil demon. How else could he have been so personally assailed?

The second dream, no less dramatic, magnified the conditions of the room in which he was sleeping, the stove breaking out of its tiled container, flaring and sparking all around him. Was it just an overstatement of the actual situation, sleeping in a room warmed by flames? No, this was too fiercely oracular. The evil demon at work again?

The third dream was more restrained, but no less affecting. Two books were lying beside his bed, one a poetry anthology, the other an encyclopaedia. They were like emissaries from another place, messages telling him he should devote his life to philosophy and science. Being of the same vision, the books coalesced into one thing: all the knowledge of humanity, the creative and the factual, could be drawn together into one coherent totality. This was the goal. This was to be his lifetime's work.

The next tutorial with the Queen, early morning as customary, included another: Ebba Sparre. She looked tired, but kept her poise, sitting straight-backed, the generous flare of her gown from the narrowest wasp waist Descartes had ever seen. Not just the youth of the girl; it seemed the Queen had employed exertions from a later time, pulling cords of a corset, one knee in the small of her back, to ensure maximum tautness.

Ebba's face was a perfect pale oval inside the array of hair that was all golden-ochre and glinting in the firelight. Christina was to talk of 'the moue from mimping of her mouth.' Ebba sat, her lissom fingers porcelain white, resting demurely on her gown. She was present under sufferance, of course, but for what purpose? To show her off? Or to have her witness the Queen's clash of swords with Europe's most eminent philosopher?

'I hope you've availed yourself of the library, especially the new volumes pillaged from Prague.'

'I have.'

'There was a good haul on the ancients.'

'I noticed, Your Highness, but not of much interest to me.'

'Mere mullock, you think?'

'No, but I find them less relevant to the present age, when the sovereignty of science and reason is paramount.'

'Example, please.'

'Consider Aristotle. I may be putting words into his mouth, but this would be a typical proposition: magnets attract iron because of their magnetic qualities.'

'Go on.'

'Well, it's a circular explanation that doesn't tell us anything.'

'But a pathetically small part of what the ancients have to offer. My librarian has shown me works by Vossius on the classics. Without this kind of learning, we're adrift.'

'It's a commendable study, but this century has seen a different kind of investigation, many advances in our knowledge of the world using observation and experiment.'

'And much bafflegab amongst it, I'll warrant. Don't you think Belle?'

Ebba was fighting sleep. The Queen's attention startled her into alertness.

'Lost among the fairy folk,' said Christina, 'and no wonder. We women are beset with too much rational sullage,'

Ebba said nothing, but must have felt chided, her attention now focused on them.

'I apologise,' said Descartes, 'much scientific study is dry. But the world is nevertheless disposed or encoded mathematically, with definite, observable patterns.'

'But how much is illusion? Think of the potsherd thrown from a kitchen window. You trace the path of the shard of clay on a grid, and it looks predictable. But take away the grid and the numbers and it's back to being random.'

Those big, ice-blue eyes again. Descartes had to tell himself to stay polite and patient.

'We use mathematics for all kinds of investigation,' he said.' Plotting the orbits of the planets, assessing the mass of objects, measuring changes in heat —'

'And how can it apply to emotion, culture and art?'

'These are vague and subjective areas of life, having no use for mathematical precision.'

'Ah, well, of course,' said Christina. 'Belle, stand for a minute.'

The Queen, approaching her in trousers, flat leather slippers and a rustic jacket the colour of mud, could not have contrasted more with Ebba, whose delicate, elegant dress and imposing height proclaimed beauty and refinement. Christina took a position behind Ebba, running her hands down the girl's slim torso, then out around the pleated swell.

'A shape, isn't it, Monsieur Descartes, and thus mathematically expressible? A means to discover the geometry of passion?'

Ebba reddened. Descartes was taken aback at this sudden swerve in subject matter. Christina, still behind the girl, cupped her hands over the tight, laced bodice.

'Each bosom, calibrated for a mathematically encoded universe. Perhaps we can calculate the volume of each soft cone of flesh?'

Christina knew he'd been ambushed and pressed her advantage:

'I find it curious, this fashion for overstating a woman's figure. To make the young into a shambling butt and the older into a waddling fustilugs. As for my Belle,' she said, 'giving her rump a slap, 'I'm all in favour.'

And so the session frittered away, until he was able to excuse himself. A globe of the world had sat on an oak table with twisted legs to one side of the fireplace during their discussion. He thought of this precision instrument and artefact, how cartographic knowledge could wrap continents around the planet. On this orb, territories unknown by far outweighed those known through exploration. Some cartographer, or their artisan, had to craft two hemispheric shells, equators precisely the same diameter.

Descartes appreciated this challenge, and the fine result of a manually-spinnable world. He ran his hand effortlessly across the Atlantic. How to stitch paper or vellum around the sphere without a wrinkle? How to apply an ink that didn't run? And what if a new land were to be discovered: would the globe-maker have to start again?

He could see Sweden, the bottom jaw of a creature about to bite Denmark, then found his exact position on the mysterious big ball.

It belonged to the Queen, but she seemed unable to appreciate the mathematics required to create it. Instead, the shift into flippancy and low humour felt like a squandering of time he could better spend asleep. Such an odd mix: irreverence, partly excused by this young mind having to find its way in the world, and all the 'Highness' one expects of a Queen. It was disconcerting, this intelligent and curious young Queen wearing the clobber of a woodsman from Njudung, or a janitor at a work-house, and speaking like one.

Kings and Queens were coerced by tradition to wear what was in keeping with their regal position, but could choose to disregard it, as Christina had done. He tried to think of her reasons: that Queenly attire was uncomfortable, that she had no interest in affirming her status through dress as the sovereign of Sweden, or that she identified more with the male gender than the female.

In the end he had to acknowledge his own prejudices: that he expected Christina to dress in finery because it was normal, it conferred status, and it added a sense of importance to the subjects discussed.

Something else about the session snagged in his mind. He would never have recalled that morning's dream of Francine, inside a log cabin, setting up a fire in the grate, were it not for Christina adding a log to the fire here at Tre Kronor.

The evil demon was never far from Descartes' locus of contemplation about the world. Any feeling that he might be deceived about something implied this trickster behind the scenes, manipulating his unsuspecting marionette. Descartes did suspect, and it wasn't from a paranoid condition but a philosopher's enquiry, intent on certainty.

If the evil genius were a master of guile and subterfuge, then the philosopher needed to examine every conviction he held, deciding whether to trust it as a fact. For many years he had questioned himself to find what was manifestly the case. This night was no different. He liked to dawdle in this area of doubt. Lying awake in the grainy darkness of his room, he tried to second-guess the frauds and feints of his adversary.

Because his feet were numbed with cold, he started there. He could neither see nor feel his feet: wasn't that evidence enough they had gone, walked away, predictably to return by morning when called again into service?

He also couldn't prove that as he lay there, awake, he was not dreaming of lying there, awake. Was there a quality distinguishing incontestably the states of dreaming and waking? If so, he couldn't pinpoint it. There were flavours, shades, frequencies or degrees of consciousness, like a piece of music that controls or shapes experience for its duration. Reveries, meditations, dreams — all related, and no clear distinction between them.

How could he be sure of the simple sum $9 \times 8 = 72$? Yes, he had the conviction, but on what was it based other than the terms of the sum itself? He might have it on good authority from other mathematicians, but the same misgivings applied: nothing in the two numbers and their multiplication produced the result other than an innate knowledge of the system in which such numbers were found and used.

Another proposition that troubled him was verifying that he had a brain. Wouldn't that be a coup for the evil genius, to make him even more of a phantom than he was already? You think because you have a brain — don't be so sure. He had never looked in a mirror while being trepanned to confirm the soggy grey organ behind his own face. Thus it was open to doubt.

He had no grounds for believing he was still in Sweden and not at the South Pole. It was certainly cold enough. It was quite conceivable he had been spirited to the opposite side of the big ball during his sleep. Nothing from sound or vision could attest to his still being in Stadsholmen, until day dawned and he woke properly to the familiarities of Tre Kronor.

He returned, as naturally as before, to the single certitude even the evil genius couldn't meddle with: I think. Though it made no difference to what he could see, Descartes closed his eyes and pictured the single word: Cogito. It had such supreme evidential power. Was it black ink on a white ground, or white letters glowing in the dark? Did the letters have serifs? No. Shouldn't it instead be the first and only word of an illuminated manuscript: divine calligraphy in pure gold?

Even in the face of this supreme certainty, the evil genius, knowing his vulnerabilities, had to have the last say. Something of the immediacy of the philosopher's situation was coming to the fore, doing its best to supersede the inviolable golden word. How do I know the evil demon hasn't orchestrated this whole mission to Sweden as a way of killing me in the cold? No, it's not the persuasions of Chanut or Freinsheim. Even Christina has been manipulated — there are thick, blood-red curtains in Tre Kronor for the sly schemer to hide behind, carrying out his malevolent plan.

Descartes preferred to avoid the court. Socialising used up precious energy, especially in futile status games, and he rarely found anyone, even among the French professors, to engage with in a meaningful way on research into astronomy, physics or optics. But once, on the hunt for warm tea to calm his sore throat, he came perilously close to the salon, and was waylaid by a Swede from a noble family, Lars Bielkes, who began with the usual pleasantries:

'I hope you're enjoying tutorials with the Queen, Monsieur Descartes.'

'Quite well.'

'Entertainment, at least, is guaranteed,' he said, tongue moistening his chapped lips.

'Correct.'

'And you've met the much-favoured Ebba Sparre?'

'I have.'

'What intrigues me is the level of intimacy between her and the Queen,' said Bielkes, pulling his sandy-coloured beard to a point.

Silence.

He continued:

'I think we all know they share a bed, but beyond that ... well, the imagination runs unbridled. One is led to surmise that the uncultured attire and manly conduct on one side and dainty, submissive girl on the other, makes of them a kind of husband and wife.'

'One is free to construe any such interpretation,' sighed Descartes, 'if the mind wants to be so occupied.'

'The pleasure-producing performance is of course of the greatest interest,' said Bielkes, his hand around the beard again, making a point. 'Doubly interesting when one is reminded of her title: Queen of the Swedes, Goths and Vandals, Princess of Finland, Duchess of Estonia and Karelia. And then —'

'If I could interrupt,' said Descartes, 'that's all quite engrossing, but I'm hoping for some tea to relieve my dry throat,' his hand at his neck for emphasis.

He entered the salon, finding a samovar in one corner where three women were deep in conversation. Facing an ice-rimed window with his cup, he could see the wiry black branches of trees outside the castle walls. They drew his mind away from Bielke's gratuitous speculations, but once he had finished the cup and soothed his throat, he caught sight of the nuisance by the main door, gazing fixedly in his direction.

Lars Bielkes was tall. It tended to put Descartes into a deferential or inferior frame of mind, though he knew it was only a difference of physique and not intellect. Shorter than most men, Descartes found himself countering this disposition of subservience, especially because Bielkes was so aloof, a haughtiness developed since his birth into an aristocratic family, all the more pronounced for his being a Swede, thus a kind of guardian for the Queen and her palace. Descartes guessed it was a moral guardianship, Bielkes automatically a Lutheran because the times dictated it, not because he had got there through assiduous study of theology.

There was no way to avoid the man, and no surprise when he was accosted once again.

'I hope you don't mind, but I have a question. You may know that here in Sweden, your reputation with regard to both Catholic and Protestant authorities in Europe precedes you.'

Descartes was losing patience with Bielkes, especially with the shift in tone.

'I would be surprised if it didn't,' he said.

'It is fair to speculate whether your move here was to escape attacks by Protestant theologians.'

'If you consult with Ambassador Chanut you will learn that I'm here by invitation from the Queen.'

'And this is my concern, as a citizen of Stadsholmen. This is a Protestant country and —'

'Before you go on, you can be assured I have no interest in converting her majesty to Catholicism. Neither is it something that interests her.'

A short scan showed Descartes many heads had turned to see if a dispute in that part of the room might escalate. The sense of a disagreement arose not from the volume of their voices but the tenor. He could imagine them believing Bielkes had issued a warning to the Catholic. Why else would they be at odds with each other? And Bielkes would be well-served by such assumptions. They would congratulate him for performing a civic duty.

'Just a warning, Monsieur Descartes,' said Bielkes, not letting go of his beard. ' I'd be on my guard.'

Descartes, avoiding eye contact, allowed him the satisfaction of the final word before striding off, his heels echoing down the hallway.

He was relieved to have poured his own tea, giving himself a piece of advice: there was every reason not to drink drinks poured by hostile hosts.

While still in the relative warmth of the palace chambers, Descartes paused at a snow-enclosed window to review another visitation by his daughter. He had been returning home in the snow through a land he had never seen before — sharp mountain peaks, vast valleys, a windmill's clanking motion of fantail mechanism, wind shaft,

spur-wheel and sack hoist, the huge vanes slicing the air above —
and inside, again, at the fireplace, there was Francine, her hinged
knees and elbows mere mechanism, her face a ceramic oval he had
fashioned himself, the body articulated for lifelike movement. But
everything was silent, the girl motionless.

He shunned that dark recess of memory, where some impulse
of grief and yearning mixed with technical know-how led him to
construct this clockwork doll. But the dream had found it and once
presented there in a remote windmill, this eerie scene frittered away.

It was all very well to suppress the memory, but wasn't it Francine and her untimely departure from the world that led him away
from overthinking, from strict analytical methods in philosophy to
more heartfelt meditations on existence?

The short walk from Tre Kronor to Ambassador Chanut's
house had to be brisk, or frozen air would deaden the extremities.
Turning through the streets, Descartes came upon older dwellings
that had survived Gustav Adolph's rebuilding programme. In high
alcoves of old blackened planking, clumped stalactites grew like
long incisors from an upper jaw. Thin ribbons of smoke rose from a
few chimneys; one house retained its turf roof where a scrawny goat
was silhouetted against the sky, its breath clouding with each bleat.

~

Morning sessions with Queen Christina continued. When he came
to join her in the light of the fire, he saw she was holding a familiar-looking manuscript. It was his *Passions of the Soul*, completed just
months before.

'I have a question. You reduce our world of feeling to just six
emotions: joy and sadness, love and hatred, wonder and desire.

What about revenge or embarrassment, what about the idleness of the loiter-sack —'

'Well...'

'The cunning of the bed-swerver? Or the lusty rompings of a hoyden?'

'Your images are comical. And the question a fair one. The range of passions are reduced, as you say. I arrived at the most salient, the most common oppositions, by intuition. What emerged were the ruling passions, not an exhaustive list.'

'You say they should be controlled, subdued.'

'By the employment of reason.'

'I can understand the wish to subdue sadness and hatred, but joy and love?'

'Governing the passions must include both the positive and negative.'

'Bumfodder,' said Christina, lifting her boot onto the upholstered tapestry of a gilded chair and leaning forward, elbow on knee. 'The passions are to be enjoyed for what they are. Think of a young buckeen tempted by the teasings of a fizgig. She's got him by the whiskery danglers and he knows it. It's the game of desire. Who'd want to rationalise it away?'

'I'm rather thinking of those who would be slaves of the passions.'

'Slaves of drink, for example? A borachio gulching a kilderkin then parbreaking all over the tavern's tables, on the road to penury and an early death.'

'Quite. The passions are all appetites of the body. I mean that while they issue from the mind, they're caused by the body. Reason, driven by resolve, keeps the mariner's wheel firm against tempests of the passions.'

'All very sober and disciplined,' said Christina,' but I don't believe a lover can be ruled by reason, or even should be.'

'It is the soul's aspiration —'

'Life and love, Monsieur Descartes. I want to ask you about Elisabeth, Princess of Bohemia. You were hoping I would offer her support?'

Descartes swallowed.

'Yes, Your Highness. She's been in very straitened circumstances.'

'But clever, I understand.'

'Yes.'

'In what did she excel?'

'Mathematics, philosophy, physics, astronomy, theology, languages.'

'You must have had a close relationship, given these . . . shared interests.'

'I was very concerned for her.'

'And young.'

Descartes could sense the hole into which he was falling. He'd listed the areas of Elisabeth's scholarship, and it was plain that a younger woman of such precocious intelligence would, at Tre Kronor, be a threat to the Queen. It was too late to downplay Elisabeth's gifts. Could he downplay his affections for her?'

'It is through your efforts and vision,' said Descartes, 'that Stadsholmen has gained such cultural eminence in Europe. Many scholars would benefit from the exchange of ideas here, and Elisabeth's education would be much enhanced —'

'I think you are in love with her.'

He could see that familiar look in her eyes, on the verge of lascivious comment.

'I have felt a responsibility for her.'

'All right, but as I said before, I don't think love and desire can be rationalised.'

'Perhaps I can be clearer,' he said, a cough rising to thwart his assurance. 'The unpleasant things of life would make a common soul unhappy, but stronger souls favour the contemplation of joy, keeping the intellect above the negative and disagreeable.'

'Do you have a child, Monsieur Descartes?'

'I had a daughter, Your Highness, but she died young.'

'I'm sorry. What was her name?'

'Francine.'

'And you have dreamt of Francine?'

'Yes.'

'Do you think dreams are subject to reason?'

'They are a category apart, but might play with what reason has disposed in the mind.'

He coughed.

'You don't sound well,' she said. 'I will get my physician to examine you.'

'My sincere thanks.'

Descartes was already a physician. He would try his own methods, but felt this ague had a will of its own.

The philosopher often imagined his beloved daughter Francine not succumbing to the illness that killed her aged five, but being looked after and given the best opportunities for education. In this alternative reality, inheriting the skills of a brilliant mathematician and philosopher, Francine learns fast, fascinated by the astonishing world around her.

Descartes has to travel alone to Stockholm for his assignment with Queen Christina. Francine, aged fourteen, remains in Holland with her mother, Helena Jans. Like her father, she is determined *to follow knowledge like a sinking star*. She needs a purpose: to find what is certain, controllable and quantifiable in the world of things. This informs her schooling for the next four years.

Using her inheritance, Francine then travels to Italy and the eminent university town of Bologna. There, at the Alma Mater Studiorum, she gains entry using her father's reputation, joining the physics department as a research assistant. An impressive array of instruments line the study chambers. She's drawn to the beautifully crafted brass telescope and microscope, with their magic portals onto the large and small. She surveys the heavens, looking for clues as to what's behind it all. She examines thin slivers of dried timber, plant filaments and pellucid layers of skin to find some hidden substructure.

From one academic year to another Francine explores, probes and investigates, unable to get to the end of either macrocosm or microcosm. She gives up, frustrated.

But what if she moves outside her father's frame of thought? Some months later she finds herself on a boat sailing from Bari to Greece. On board is a man of about her father's age, simply dressed, with few possessions. He has an astuteness in his bearing, conveyed too by his penetrating gaze and well-modulated voice. They start talking about the wind and weather, the tides and the waxing moon. What he says doesn't sound convincing to her exacting, mathematical mind — it's all about processes with no start or end, about constant change and flow, about rejecting details in favour of the widest perspective.

Francine describes her quest to find answers. She has eyes to see, but even the ingenious instruments at the university couldn't get her any closer to her goal. Was she looking in the wrong place?

The sage, if that's what he was, contemplates her question for some time, then says:
What you are looking for is what is looking.

───❦───

Though it was unheated, Descartes would return to the library involuntarily, drawn by habit, by the meditative communion with words so deeply ingrained in him. Freinsheim's absence meant it was quieter: he could be on his own for long periods.

He entered through an arched doorway in oak with three crowns carved into the upper curve. It might have been an illusion, a bird blotting the sun for a moment, a steward or menial in fleeting exit after idling in the library, but he half-sensed an observer. Or was it stalker? Bielkes perhaps, seeking information on what the philosopher was reading? Or wanting to get him alone to threaten him in a place with no witnesses?

Descartes's skin prickled at his neck. Were there marauders at Tre Kronor, or was it just his fear? Slowly, warily, he made a tour of the shelves, peered into dark corners and alcoves. No-one, yet.

He waited ten minutes, fifteen, then could start to read, the outer world dissolving, just the smell of leather and polished wood. It was in one of these reveries, quiet but for the light wheeze from his windpipe, that he reached for a sparsely stitched volume in faded vellum on a high shelf and promptly dropped it. Bending to retrieve it, he noticed one of the pages was misaligned and ready to fall out. The volume included various botanical specimens, many from distant lands, accurately and lovingly drawn. This page gone aslant was engraved with a fruit, the name *cucumus* referring to the cantaloupe cultivated in sunny Spain. This furrowed specimen grew in the Tuscan hills where Freinsheim was probably lounging.

Descartes was transfixed by the picture. Surely it was just a coincidence, finding this image of the same fruit that rose from nowhere to occupy his dream thirty years before? As a mathematician, he knew such things could coincide, given the play of random events over time: how could something of such personal significance otherwise be accounted for? Or was the evil genius at work again, teasing him with this intersection of matching symbols? Was this the portent or shadowy presence, his nemesis haunting the passageways of Tre Kronor's library, waiting the chance to spring such a surprise?

This, then, was no threat from the evil genius, but something more like a provocation: *Try explaining this one, Monsieur Descartes.*

Down a wide hallway of Tre Kronor, Descartes recognised Oxenstierna coming towards him. There was no-one else. The tall figure with his slow, measured gait and priestly bearing moved into shadow, then was side-lit from an arched window, before being veiled in shadow once again. They met near a portrait of the Queen's grandfather, Karl IX, the tempera on panel catching light of fifty years before that was reduced to one point in the king's eye.

'I remember him,' said the Chancellor. 'Those features were passed down to Gustav Adolf, then Queen Christina.'

'About the line of succession?' asked Descartes. 'You asked me once if I thought the Queen would marry. Could I request your opinion on the matter?'

It was better to suggest the official, not the personal, to feign naiveté, than risk talk of Christina's sexuality. Oxenstierna seemed to visibly age.

'There was a possibility, when her cousin Karl Gustav returned from travel nine years ago. A good-looking young man, the Queen quite taken with him. It was the talk of the court, word spreading of a royal connection. But I was against the match. Christina was only fifteen, not of legal age. It was a good excuse. Karl Gustav's palatine family only wanted to widen their power.'

The Chancellor was looking out across Tre Kronor's spires, squinting into the distance.

'I needn't have worried, as it happened. Christina was enamoured of him, but had no intention of going to the altar. You might say she enjoyed the game, and employed delaying tactics: that they should wait till her coronation, still three years away; that he should think of his army career . . .'

The memory brought a wry grin to the Chancellor's face, the first time Descartes had seen it.

'You can't help being a patriarch to the Queen. I'm thinking of statecraft, and . . .'

Oxenstierna saved him from the dead-end.

'It could have worked, at one time, when she was younger. But affairs of state became competitive, then belligerent. In my military career I've grown used to hostilities but . . . not this kind.'

'I'm sorry to hear that.'

The Chancellor sighed.

'Reigning monarchs die and hand on the crown. Who knows what Sweden will be like in fifty years? Or three hundred?'

There was a pause, then his attention fixed on Descartes and out came one of his typical directives:

'You should get that chest seen to.'

Wise advice. His breathing was like the sound of wind rushing through a forest.

It was a more unusual item among the spoils of war: a lion. Sitting in a cage not large enough to walk in a circle, the beast's leonine countenance was permanently crestfallen. Unnaturally thin, his only protection against the Stadsholmen winter was a moulting mane. Constant refrigeration would certainly kill the animal; it was only a matter of when.

Descartes, having never seen one of the big cats, was fascinated by the way its wasting body was setting the bones and muscle into sharp relief. He could see the prehensile claws, the trochanter nub of the femur and spina scapulae he had identified in smaller cats during his dissection work in Paris.

One of the French professors had joined him in this annex of the castle. While Descartes peered in between the bars, his eye following every contour of the feline form, the professor stayed at one remove.

'I think I've seen enough,' he said.

'No, this is intriguing,' said Descartes, almost to himself.

'That look in the poor beast's eye: a stupor, like he's dead already.'

'Oh, no matter,' said Descartes, circling the cage. 'The wasting of muscles gives a rare overview of the skeletal form.'

'You make the creature into a mere machine.'

'It is. Automatic motion of a physiological organism.'

'There's nary a hint of motion in this one.'

'Probably a poor diet,' said Descartes.

'How do you know? This cat can discriminate, or how could it decide what is prey and what's not?'

'The cat simply perceives prey and pursues it. Unlike us, it is not aware of having perceptual states.'

The professor barely heard Descartes' last comment. The latch of the gate could be heard, then silence . . . leaving the philosopher with the lion.

The Queen had been contemplating Descartes' theory of mind and body. He had spoken to her of another reality behind the mundane one of a hundred courtiers, cooks, guards, guests, stewards and ostlers. It was a hundred presences, each with its unique and invisible glow, living and moving in Tre Kronor's wood-panelled rooms, under its ornately-plastered ceilings.

'What you called this vexed issue has kept me awake.'

'I apologise, Your Highness.'

'There's no need. I wanted a thinker, not a proverb-monger, and I have one.'

'I'll do my best to clarify.'

'Are we to take it that the body is extended but the mind is unextended?'

'A mysterious co-existence, but yes.'

'Two different substances in one person?'

'Correct. One is a substance that will die and decay, and the other transcends the physical realm.'

'How can you be sure it transcends the physical?'

'Because, firstly, it is not in space, being both everywhere in acts of observation near and far, and nowhere in particular. Secondly, it is not tied to the present. It is yesterday by memory, tomorrow by anticipation, and neither of these in the imagination.'

'And thirdly?'

He sensed impatience and irony in her question.

'And thirdly it can't be broken into parts the way a body can.'

'My head hurts.'

'I'm sorry Your Highness. It may help that we have two different faculties for investigation. Science is based on careful observation, guided by mathematical principles. But we also have innate ideas, not tied to the senses.'

'And these come from God?'

'Yes, from deep in our nature. One such idea is that there is a material world, of oceans and trees, rainbows, ships and bridges, princes and thieves —'

'Mangy milksops and scurvy scum.'

'Quite. And I have long believed there is some scheming trickster bent on deceiving us, on playing games with our minds.'

'The enemy within?'

'Well, one that would make a dupe of us.'

'See how we're beset by flam and fellness.'

'We are.'

'I can hear a rasp in your breathing. You should have a rest.'

Descartes didn't need reminding of the effort needed to lift his lungs. The gurgle of coagulum couldn't be ignored. The Queen suggested he remain by the fire while she met with Chancellor Oxenstierna on state matters. The man arrived in the chamber with the usual confidence, this time wearing a robe lined in ermine fur and with a sheaf of papers in his gnarled hand. Christina's eyes rolled.

The philosopher hadn't been dismissed yet, no doubt because she wouldn't have the Chancellor overrule her. Oxenstierna winced as he walked, as if last night's suckling pig or chilled apples disagreed with him. A mulligrubs problem, as the Queen would say.

'Monsieur Descartes will remain here,' she said to the wall.

'Then we will confer in the state room.'

'Your wish is my remand.'

As they turned to go she had time for a sly smile.

Descartes had nodded off when the Queen returned with a question she said was dominating her mind throughout discussions of state affairs.

'This strange relationship between mind and body; if some fat-gut chooses by force of will to moderate his scoffing, his body might thank him and live another ten years. And a starveling who decides to shovel sweetmeats down his gullet might likewise live another ten years. So the mind affects the body and the two cannot be as separate as you describe.'

'You're right, there is a reciprocal relation between soul and body.'

'And some knuff with blains and scabs offending the sight of townsfolk might feel their disgust, and so obstruct the health of his soul?'

'Yes. Better he tries to override those repelled by his appearance.'

'So for the corny-face, his well-being reduces to a state of mind?'

'It will relax his heart and improve circulation.'

'Couldn't that apply to your own condition? Are you able to conquer the ague with a determined state of mind?'

'To a degree, Your Highness. But some diseases will find their own way, so even the strongest souls must relent.'

'You're a physician, and seek to preserve life.'

'True. This is the intention.'

'But in the end the body fails completely.'

'And frees the soul. Instead of looking for ways to preserve life, I've found an easier, surer way. Not to fear death.'

He sensed the threat from a distance: shadows moving, a strategy of attack. But the cause? Why him?

They've come for me, was the surmise, his adversaries catching up with him, as he suspected, in the library. It was Bielkes, with two stooges materialising from the dark either side of him, their eye sockets like paired caves under the overhead light. Somehow they had backed him into an alcove of books stacked to head height.

Looking down, Descartes could see a gold crucifix hanging on his own chest from a plaited leather thong. Bielkes saw it too, coming in closer to observe the evidence. Descartes knew the cross was just a costume item for the Queen's ballet: it shouldn't be taken seriously. But Bielkes' advance was steady, deliberate, his forearm coming up, clamping the Catholic dissenter against the doors of an enclosed bookcase behind him. It was hard to breathe,

'We won't have our Queen preached to by a flattering agent of popery,' said Bielkes, his leering face just inches away.

Descartes felt several responses vying for utterance, but could hardly draw breath. He felt himself starting to asphyxiate, and thought: Is this to be my death, at the hands of religious fanatics? No, I don't fear death, but strangulation is a horrible way to —

He jumped back into wakefulness, throat clogged with phlegm, and let loose several painful coughs into a handkerchief as the first greyness of dawn seeped in through a slit in the curtains.

Having seen such squeamishness when one of the French scholars beheld a caged beast, Descartes wondered if, as a breed, they were out of touch with the real world. The Queen had welcomed them into Tre Kronor with gifts purchased from the royal coffers. She had bought this erudition of intellectuals to establish Stadsholmen as a centre of high culture. Descartes was inclined to call them a pedantry of scholars; Oxenstierna, very likely, an 'expensive intrusion.'

Descartes had to admit he was one of their number, but could at least separate himself by appearance. He dressed smartly in black, his wigs plain and not a mass of plumped-up curls. He eschewed buckles and bows, hated the fussy filigree of lace at throat and cuff, and would never be seen in plumage. That was for strutting peacocks, or in the Queen's vocabulary, simpering meacocks.

She wouldn't defame her purchased professors in this way, but it hadn't escaped Descartes' cognisance that four large mirrors in the salon were in almost constant use, the overdressed men checking and admiring their frippery and fandangle, parading their own hauteur of intellectual accomplishment and practising flowery gestures of obeisance or salutation.

This irked the Swedish courtiers, who saw them as leeches sucking the lifeblood of the Swedish state. Descartes was convinced Christina cared little about the drain on financial resources. Following the Chancellor's confessions, it seemed certain the invited guests were part of the Queen's armoury against him, a show of achievement, knowledge and acumen at odds with Oxenstierna's mundane politics.

But the Chancellor may have realised one thing, of which the Queen was probably unaware. It was the professors' duty to attend Academy sessions over which the Queen presided. The consistent view, Descartes learned, was one of tedium. Christina chose the topics, steered the discussion, and bored the participants. Many made excuses to avoid attendance, illness being the most common.

Christina wasn't lacking in discernment. Descartes wondered if she did in fact know her guests' opinion of the Academy, but persevered to save face. Her role was one of authority, and in front of the professors this had to be backed up with competence in languages, science and philosophy. She couldn't expect to be the equal of those around her, but must still hold sway. It was quite a trial. Princess

Elisabeth, being so young and brilliant, would have been a formidable adversary for Christina, not just in the range of disciplines but depth of knowledge. No wonder there was no progress in bringing her to Sweden.

He had to admit the Queen was in this circumstance by birth, and he knew her relative immaturity and quirks of character. She needed self-confidence, but, understandably, lacked it. She was intelligent, but not as gifted as Elisabeth. Descartes could engage with Elisabeth virtually as an equal, while tutoring Christina from a sense of duty. He had to be even-handed about this. Though he found the Queen's engagement to be keen but superficial, she had an honesty about her. He could see someone genuinely interested in the world, but hidebound by her position.

Now, lying in bed at Ambassador Chanut's house, chest almost too heavy to lift with his congested lungs, he thought of Francine. Had she chosen the scene of each encounter: the meadow and river, the hearth in a log cabin, the hearth in a windmill? If so, how could she dispose them in his mind? And why the fireplace? Was it a point of focus or energiser, or was it the Queen and her discussions around the fire that kept installing such tropes into his sleep? Why this increased frequency of Francine's presence: could she sense his imminent approach?

With every day he was more certain — this arctic mission was the denouement of his life. Images drifted past him: the voyage among Baltic bergs, the farcical ballet, icicles bared at him like crystal fangs, the great muscular machine of a couchant lion . . . and then this strange young Queen, too restless, unformed and worldly for her cold northern castle, too unsuited to the image of a gracious monarch with glittering crown, decorated in the collars and cuffs of an exorbitant courtly gown.

Before drifting into sleep his mind returned to Mersenne's salon in France, to a heated discussion with Thomas Hobbes on colours and optics, and the woman who sat in on that session, listening intently, who did suit all that adornment of costume: Margaret Cavendish.

Unlike the preening foreign courtiers at Tre Kronor, the arrogance of their apparel matching the arrogance of their assertions, Margaret Cavendish was restrained and discriminating in her observations, but to the eye would outshine them all. They were interesting aspects of the lady to reconcile: a modesty that preserved her virtue, and a costume that belied it.

~

Affected by congested lungs, his only recourse in waking hours was to distract himself with work, writing statutes for the Swedish Royal Academy.

There was a new sound to his chest, something slushy like shellfish sizzling in oil. He had to bear these corrupted lungs to an audience with the Queen, along with the completed statutes for the Royal Academy, with the sense that, as a guest, his end of the bargain had been fulfilled.

But Descartes was too ill to attend his next tutorial, sending an apologetic message from Chanut's house where he was staying. He prescribed himself a compound of wine and tobacco in the hope of coughing up coagulum.

The only advantage of his condition was confinement to a warm bed. He sat up, facing a vertical strip of dim light from the gap in two heavy velvet curtains, finding his mind preoccupied with something intriguing but irrational: the three young women who had influenced his life more differently and deeply than any male friend or colleague.

Princess Elisabeth had led him to abandon earlier theories that women's emotional nature meant they were less rational and only of scientific interest.

His lost child Francine, came back to him in dreams. What did this signify? It must be that her non-physical (now disembodied) spirit, which he had proved of himself and must also apply to his daughter, was drawn to him. Or he was drawn to her. What tested his powers of reasoning was whether his deeper self was really playing with her in that dream of the rope swing in the Netherlands. Had they together created a psychic space where father and child could interact, soul to soul? His dreams were a raw material, direct and unadulterated. They said Francine was much more than just an imagined object. What could it mean that Descartes and Francine could have highly affecting nocturnal encounters when one was asleep and the other dead?

Third was Queen Christina, his attitude to her a mix of respect (dictated by protocol), curiosity and exasperation.

Falsely confident the wine and tobacco had had a salutary effect, Descartes ordered a coach for the next day's early morning tutorial.

Official business was over in a minute. Descartes handed the Queen the finished statute manuscripts and she passed them to Ebba Sparre, who sat on a low chair, silent, her ringlets shining. This morning she had the attractive power of an exquisite flower, her dress in purple damask like an inverted bell of petals. Christina, as usual, was direct.

'It saddens me that Stadsholmen may have given you this morbid condition.'

'I shan't blame the city, Your Highness. The mechanism we talked about is faltering, and will succumb to the laws governing matter.'

'You're very sanguine about it.'

This, he realised, would be his last audience with the young Queen. It felt strange, death absolving him of any further tutelage. His next comment was more diplomatic than truthful:

'Much of our discussion has been ... refreshingly light-hearted.'

'Then levity should be added to your account of the passions?'

'It may be a category all on its own, for another work. Life as a brief carnival of fools, though I don't mean —'

'You were going to excuse the gentilesse? They're as much loobies, churls and saddle-geese as the rest of them. Better that our dialogues should have been, though instructive, a comedy.'

It was a softening in the Queen's demeanour. He said:

'I sense in Your Highness someone who, more than being instructed by another, has taught herself, from books.'

'You're correct.'

'I did the same. Early schooling showed me one important thing: that even after years of tuition, I was ignorant. So I educated myself.'

'In scripture as well?'

'Yes, er ... to a degree.'

'But your thought is not circumscribed by Catholic faith?'

'I think that's a fair summation.'

'Don't fret. While I'm on the throne Catholics will enjoy equal rights as any Lutheran bonehead or bible-batterer.'

'I'm relieved to hear it Your Majesty.'

'Tell me more about your self-education.'

'First, what you already know. The querent's need for much reading and conjecture. Next is the oven, going to bed and allowing thoughts of the day some heat treatment. In the morning they've risen as fully-formed ideas.'

'And has Tre Kronor been a good oven?'

'Sweden's winter darkness promotes this inwardness, but the cold works in the opposite direction, paralysing cogitation.'

Ebba remained still, composed.

Christina nodded, her wide eyes taking in the philosopher's pallid face, the laborious heave of his chest. For a moment Descartes saw neither Queen nor student, but a counterpart, perhaps a friend, perhaps even a daughter.

Her escape from the silence and weight of that moment, of connection, was into the frivolous.

'We have something important in common, I think.'

'What is that Your Highness?'

'Our noses. They are ... what's the correct word ...'

'Illustrious?'

'Yes, that will suffice. Long and large, but certainly not the snouts of a sniff-shit.'

'Aristocratic?'

'Yes. And prying. We poke them into other's business, telling the pawky from the noddy-peak.'

'And thereby discover more about the world.'

It was a forced line and he knew it. There were personal things floating around them in that part of the chamber, quivering the candles, making the usually imperturbable Ebba fidget. The Queen, too, knew this would be the last session, that he would die in Sweden, but couldn't manage sympathetic expression. He said:

'You are young, Your Highness, and still have this extraordinary world to explore. I am at the other end. Still, death always seems too soon. You may remember I had declared myself unafraid of death, which is fine until its actual approach. We've discussed philosophy, but have never touched on this ultimate background. The solution to the enigma of the world lies beyond it, so our discussions and their conclusions must always be unfinished.'

'But I didn't want them to finish,' said Christina.

He could see a tear join the sheen of her eye, ready to fall at the eyelid's brim.

After that last audience Descartes went into a rapid decline.

Never giving up his meditative disposition, on his death bed it is easy to imagine his thoughts as he is unable to resist the scree-slope descent, then the brink, the free-fall.

He has renounced, finally, the automated puppet of Francine as an empty plaything. He wants her non-physical essence, because he believes the soul is unrestricted. And even in the final moments it is just as dynamic, steadfastly reconfiguring itself.

I am, primarily, thought. My body is dying, has died.

So saith the ghost.

More compelling reading

Small presses rely on the support of readers to tell others about the books they enjoy. To support this book and its author, we ask you to consider placing a review on the site where you bought it. Other books by Hugh Major include three award-winning non-fiction works:

The Lantern in the Skull: Consciousness and marginal zones of the extraordinary (Attar Books, 2019)
Finalist: Best Book, 2020 Ashton Wylie Awards
Finalist: Best Book, 2020 International Independent Book Awards

"*The Lantern In The Skull* offers an engaging meditation on consciousness, that clear light that seemingly lives inside your head, stubbornly resisting materialistic explanations. Author Hugh Major provides a clearly written and well-informed study of the increasingly critical need to see beyond a simple clockwork model of reality." — Dean Radin PhD, chief scientist at the Institute of Noetic Sciences, author of *Entangled Minds and The Noetic Universe*

A camera previously in perfect working order, which inexplicably won't photograph a fetish in an African village chief's basement, provides the first stop on Hugh Major's engaging survey. Using his own experiences as a springboard, he considers telepathy, psychic perceptions, psychedelic insights, artistic transports, near death experiences, and much else.

Human consciousness is sufficiently elastic to accommodate all these experiences. Yet the nature of consciousness itself is a conundrum, and the evidence for marginal experiences remains contentious. Hugh

Major provides a timely snapshot of current research into "marginal zones of the extraordinary". In precise, jargon-free language, he indicates the territory being explored and outlines major directions researchers are travelling. There are numerous captivating, and surprising, discoveries along the way.

From Monkey to Moth: An imaginal evolution (Papawai Press, 2016)
Runner-Up: Best Unpublished Manuscript, 2016 Ashton Wylie Awards

"Very readable, eclectic, full of wisdom drawn from experience. The ineffable is given shape with allegory, parable and metaphor. I so enjoyed it I went back several times to the sections that aroused a wealth of feeling." — Joy Cowley ONZ, DCNZN, OBE, author of *Veil Over The Light: Selected Spiritual Writings* and *Navigation, A Memoir*

Notes on the Mysterium Tremendum (Papawai Press, 2013)
Finalist: Best Book, 2013 Ashton Wylie Awards

"A profound and fascinating introduction to the universe as inner experience as well as outer reality." — Ashton Wylie judges' report

"What this book is actually about is those mysterious connections between the physical world and the myriad intangibles that we all wonder about and question."— Janine McVeagh, *Te Awa, The River*

Also from Attar Books

Two compelling memoirs from anthropologist and artist Judith Hoch. With her husband, John, Judith built a house in at the edge of a rain forest in New Zealand's South Island. They also frequently travelled to Miami, Florida, where Judith taught for years and where friends and family lived. Each of Judith's memoirs focus on one of her two homes.

Prophecy on the River by Judith Hoch (Attar Books, 2019)
Finalist: Best Book, 2020 Ashton Wylie Awards
Finalist: Best Book, 2020 International Independent Book Awards

Lights with no apparent source, heating her back while she walks along a riverbank, initiate American anthropologist Judith Hoch into a decades-long process of spiritual renewal. In this vivid prose, Judith describes what happens when she and her husband struggle to restore newly-purchased New Zealand land to native forest. It quickly becomes a spiritual as well as ecological task — and proves far more difficult than she ever anticipated.

"Judith Hoch describes her magical experiences with the people, land and history of New Zealand. Written in graceful, eloquent prose, this memoir tells how Hoch came to recognise in a very heartfelt and visceral way that her own spiritual rejuvenation, along with that of both indigenous Māori people and descendants of the colonial settlers, depends upon acquiring deep respect for rivers and forests, and appreciating the innate power of the natural world and its need for revitalization. Her story is compelling, the narrative flows easily, and the overall experience is both moving and motivating." — Richard Schwartz, Emeritus Professor, Florida International University

Soul Healing in Afro-Cuban Miami by Judith Hoch (Attar Books, 2025)

Judith Hoch's follow-up to *Prophecy on the River* describes the insights she gained from her experiences with Lucumí, the Afro-Cuban spiritual practice also known as Santería that flourishes underground in Miami. Her book recounts extraordinary rituals performed by a gifted Lucumí diviner that helped her understand herself better, resolve longstanding issues with her family, and receive life-changing guidance that facilitated her personal growth. A flamboyantly written, often startling story, that reveals the sacred workings of this much maligned but secretly celebrated pathway to the spirit world. And a story that takes us into the heart of family discord, only to lift the reader into life-affirming heights.

Interrogations: Selected writing 1976–1990 by Keith Hill (Disjunct Books, 2024)

Interrogations presents the best of Hill's early writing to showcase fourteen years of literary, cultural and spiritual exploration. Inspired by traditional poetic forms and the avant-garde, drawing on influences that range from Blake to Beckett, Rumi to Jarry, Mirabai to Artaud, Bashō to Bly, Hill's work interrogates key myths that have shaped Western culture. Displaying a seriously irreverent sense of humour, leaping from mystic idealism to sly satire, this collection will delight readers with its probing critiques, surprising genre shifts and visionary daring.

'A unique creative individual who has produced a huge body of distinctive work. In New Zealand literature there's no one quite like him.'
— Roger Horrocks

'Keith Hill engages with spiritual issues from both an artistic and a scholarly perspective, an invaluable combination at a time when questions of meaning and identity trouble people living in a postmodern world riven with conundrums and complexities. A singular writer.'
— Peter Dornauf

'Keith Hill's existentially-sharp writings cut away the excess to reveal an essential spiritual journey undertaken with sincerity and wisdom.'
— Richard von Sturmer